Match Wits with The Hardy Boys®!

Collect the Original
Hardy Boys Mystery Stories®
by Franklin W. Dixon

Celebrate 60 Years with the World's Greatest Super Sleuths!

THE WAILING SIREN MYSTERY

CAUGHT in their motorboat the *Sleuth,* by a sudden storm at sea, Frank and Joe Hardy are helpless when the engine conks out. Drifting farther from shore amid the tumultuous waves, the boys are relieved to see the lights of a yacht. But their SOS is ignored.

The shrill sound of a siren fills the night air. Moments later, a helicopter drops an object alongside the *Sleuth.* To the young detectives' astonishment it proves to be a wallet containing two thousand dollars.

The next day their close pal Chet Morton rushes to the Hardys' home to report that the Morton farm truck carrying a shipment of high-powered rifles belonging to his uncle, a big-game hunter, has been stolen.

These two apparently unconnected events are clues in a tangle of mystery which turns out to be one of the detective brothers' most exciting adventures.

"Stand where you are!" the man ordered

The Hardy Boys Mystery Stories®

THE
WAILING SIREN
MYSTERY

BY

FRANKLIN W. DIXON

GROSSET & DUNLAP
Publishers • New York
A member of The Putnam & Grosset Group

PRINTED ON RECYCLED PAPER

CONTENTS

CHAPTER I

Money from the Sky

THE *Sleuth* roared toward Barmet Bay as fast as its propeller could churn the sullen sea. At its wheel sat Joe Hardy, tensely watching the black clouds. His brother Frank bent anxiously over the throbbing motor.

"Think we'll make it?" Joe asked.

"If the engine holds out. Listen! It's missing again!"

The motor coughed. At the same time a jagged bolt of lightning flung itself from a towering thunderhead. It was followed by a deafening crash. As rain poured down on the boys in blinding sheets, the engine suddenly conked out.

"We're in for it!" Frank called.

"What's the matter?"

"It could be the gas line."

Frank opened the hatch to the engine, grabbed the toolbox, and set to work. Without power, the

1

Sleuth was in danger of being capsized by the giant waves.

"I'll try to keep her heading into the wind," Joe shouted.

The storm had broken in all its fury. Lightning flashed almost continuously, and the air reverberated to the roll of thunder. One blinding flash hit the water not far from the boat.

"Wow!" Joe exclaimed. "A little closer and we would have had it!"

"Never saw a storm come up so fast," Frank said.

The Hardys, high school boys out for an evening cruise in their motorboat, had gone farther into the ocean from Barmet Bay than usual. Dark-haired Frank, tall, slender, and keen-witted, was worried. Joe, a year younger, with blond, wavy hair and an impetuous nature, was not too concerned as yet.

This trait of Joe's was responsible for their present predicament. Joe had listened to only the first half of the late-afternoon weather report. Now the two boys were caught in the center of a heavy summer squall.

Frothy whitecaps slapped over the side of the boat as it rocked dangerously in the turbulent sea. The ponchos that the boys had grabbed out of a locker gave them some protection from the rain, but their slacks and sneakers were becoming soaked. And the Barmet Bay inlet, with its blinking beacons, seemed to be drifting away from the *Sleuth* at an alarming rate.

"How's it coming?" Joe called.

"No luck yet. If this storm keeps up, Mother will be a wreck. You know how she worries about us being out here in bad weather."

"And Aunt Gertrude isn't helping her any," Joe added. "She's probably telling Mother of the perils of the sea and why boys shouldn't have motorboats."

"I wish Dad were home to calm them," Frank said. "Did he say when he was coming back from Washington?"

"No," Joe replied. "He never can tell how long his secret government cases are going to last."

"I wonder what it's about this time. Dad said we might be of some help to him in—"

Frank was interrupted by another large wave which struck the *Sleuth* with a resounding whack.

As Joe pulled hard on the wheel to avoid an avalanche of water, he cried out, "Frank, look!"

In the distance a yacht was bobbing up and down in the giant waves.

"Maybe the captain will help us out," Frank suggested. "Let's signal."

He picked up a flashlight and beamed an S O S, hoping to attract attention. There was no response. The *Sleuth* was evidently too low in the water for the signal to be seen.

In a matter of minutes it was completely dark

on the water. The lightning and thunder ceased, but the rain and heavy wind continued.

The motor of the *Sleuth* was still dead. Frank had been unable to locate the trouble with the craft rocking so violently. The use of tools was out of the question.

Suddenly Joe shouted, "Frank, the yacht's heading this way. She'll run us down!"

Frantically Joe signaled with his flashlight. A moment later the winking lights of the ship were blotted out.

Hearts beating wildly, the boys waited. If the ship came closer without seeing them, there would be only one thing for them to do—jump overboard!

Suddenly the boys saw the yacht's lights again. They were farther away than before.

"Whew!" said Frank in relief.

"I think I hear a helicopter," Joe said. "Let's signal again."

Above the roar of the wind and the breakers came the sound of whirling rotors.

"That pilot's crazy to be out in a storm like this," said Joe.

"Maybe he's lost. From the sound, he must be circling. But I can't see him."

"Nor I. Hope he doesn't think the light on the yacht is a landing field," Joe said with a shudder.

At that moment the wail of a siren filled the air. "Where's that coming from?" Joe asked.

"She'll run us down!" Joe shouted

"Either the copter or the yacht," Frank reasoned. "The sound couldn't carry this far from shore in the storm."

The yacht's deck lights blazed again. Then, as before, they disappeared.

"What's going on?" Joe asked.

"Wish I knew."

Clear vision was cut off by the blinding rain. Five minutes, ten minutes went by. The rotors could be heard faintly.

Then suddenly the sounds of the helicopter became clearer again. Within a matter of seconds the craft was directly overhead. As the boys looked up, there was a swishing sound, then a smack on the water directly alongside the *Sleuth*. Leaning way over, Frank just managed to grasp an object as it was about to sink beneath the waves.

"What is it?" Joe asked.

"Feels like a wallet! And a fat one too."

Focusing his flashlight on the billfold, Frank whistled. "It's full of money!"

CHAPTER II

Two Losses

JOE's eyes popped at the sight of the bulging wallet. "It must have dropped from the helicopter—but why, is more than I can figure out," he muttered.

Frank exclaimed, "Hundred-dollar bills!" As he started to count them, Joe shouted, "Hang on!"

A big wave was bearing down on them. It hit the craft broadside, tilting it and throwing Frank and Joe into the churning water. Automatically they struggled out of their ponchos.

Despite the predicament they were in, Frank and Joe kept their heads. Being sons of Fenton Hardy, the famous detective, they had been well schooled in meeting perilous situations.

Starting with the mystery of *The Tower Treasure,* they had had many narrow escapes tracking down criminals. Their latest case, known as *The Secret of the Lost Tunnel,* had taken them to the

South on the trail of Civil War gold. But now they realized that the elements could be as dangerous as the craftiest of criminals.

Spluttering and struggling, Frank and Joe fought their way toward the *Sleuth*. Though expert swimmers, they had all they could do to overtake it.

Joe was the first to grasp the side of the boat. With eyes smarting and head spinning, he hauled himself over the gunwale.

Then Frank hoisted one leg over the side and tumbled into the bottom of the boat.

"Did—did you lose the wallet?" Joe asked.

Frank held up the dripping wallet. A quick flip showed the money was still there. They could count it later. Frank put it in his pocket.

The rain had stopped, and visibility was better. The yacht was now in sight, but moving rapidly southward.

"It made a quick getaway," Frank remarked. "Wonder where it's going."

While Joe bailed out the boat with a large can from the locker, Frank continued his work on the motor and repaired it quickly.

"Try the starter, Joe."

The motor roared into action. One danger was over, although it would still require skillful piloting to make the inlet.

"I'm curious about that wallet," Joe said as they plowed along through the stormy sea.

"I think I'll count it." Frank beamed his flashlight on the bills and thumbed through them.

"How much?" Joe asked eagerly.

"Two thousand dollars!" Frank exclaimed. "And not a mark of identification in the wallet."

Joe grinned. "We'll have a sweet time finding the owner."

"He might not want to be found," Frank said slowly. "Maybe it's stolen money."

The boys continued to speculate about the wallet until they neared the mouth of the inlet. Then conversation ceased while Joe put all his energy into the task of keeping the *Sleuth* on a straight course.

Joe took a bearing on the blinker of the entrance buoy, and in five minutes the turbulent ocean was behind them.

"Neat navigating!" Frank commented as he looked at the lights of Bayport twinkling in the distance.

When the *Sleuth* finally came to the Hardys' boathouse, Joe cut the motor. Frank leaped out and secured the line.

Two men entered the side door of the boathouse. Frank recognized them as Detective Smuff and Patrolman Con Riley of the Bayport Police Department.

"Where have you two been?" Smuff shouted.

"Why? Were you looking for us? Anything wrong at home?" Frank asked.

"No," said Riley. "But see here, you've been lost. Didn't you know it?"

"Who sent out the alarm for us?" Frank asked.

"Your mother."

"Lock up, Joe, while I telephone home," Frank directed.

He ran halfway down the block to a drugstore. After telephoning Mrs. Hardy that they were safe, he hurried back to Joe. Then the boys drove home in their convertible.

Mrs. Hardy flung open the front door and hugged her sons as they came in. She was a petite woman, with a pretty face and wavy hair. Frank and Joe bent down to kiss her.

"Thank goodness you're safe!" she exclaimed.

"It was rough going for a while," Joe said, putting an arm around his mother's shoulder. "But we ran into what may turn out to be a big mystery."

"What was that? Another mystery?" The voice belonged to Aunt Gertrude, unmarried sister of Mr. Hardy, who lived at their home. She came bustling down the stairs. "Well, you keep out of it!"

Tall, angular Aunt Gertrude was a very energetic person. She felt that her chief mission in life was to protect her nephews from the dangers involved in their mysteries, especially when their father was away from home.

While the boys changed into dry clothes, Mrs.

Hardy prepared sandwiches and milk. As they ate, Aunt Gertrude plied them with questions. They told of their strange experience during the storm —the yacht that had vanished so suddenly, the helicopter, the wailing siren, and finally the wallet.

Mrs. Hardy and Aunt Gertrude gasped in amazement. "Two thousand dollars!"

"And it fell right out of the sky with no identification," Frank explained.

"Nothing good will come of this," Aunt Gertrude predicted. "Get rid of it right away. Some cutthroat will come here to recover it."

"We'll take the wallet and money to police headquarters," Frank said.

The boys hurried to headquarters. Smuff and Riley were there, reporting to Police Chief Collig about the safe return of the Hardys.

When Smuff and Riley left, Frank handed the wallet to Collig and told about the helicopter.

The chief said he would send out a teletype notice of "a large sum of money found near Bayport," and hope for a quick response.

Curious to hear whether the message had brought forth any claimants, Frank telephoned Collig after breakfast the next morning. There was no news.

Joe suggested to Frank that they drive to Bayport Airport. On reaching the administration building there, Frank asked the airport security chief if any pilot had mentioned losing anything from a plane the night before.

"Last night, you say? Nobody was up in that storm."

"We heard a helicopter."

"It wasn't from here," the man said. "And no one landed during the storm."

The boys telephoned two other airports in the vicinity and received the same answer. As the Hardys drove back to the city, Frank said:

"It's my guess the chopper was a private one."

"That still doesn't explain why the wallet fell out," Joe mused. "And it's pretty certain the owner wouldn't expect to recover the money from the ocean. What do you think we ought to do about it?"

"I think we should put an ad in the newspaper," Frank replied. "Let's stop at the *News* on the way home."

When they reached the office of the *Bayport News*, Frank filled out a form and handed it to the classified ad clerk. The advertisement read:

Found: Wallet near Bayport. Contains sum of money. Owner identify and write Q.E.D., Box 22, News Office.

"I hope this lands the real owner," Joe said on the way home, "and not a lot of phonies."

The boys had just finished eating lunch when

they heard someone run up the front porch steps. A second later the doorbell rang frantically.

Frank opened the door. The boys' overweight friend Chet Morton raced in. From his flushed face and heaving chest it was evident that he had run a long distance.

"Frank! Joe!" he shouted. "You've got to help me quick!"

"What's the matter?"

"We've been robbed! Somebody stole our truck! All my uncle's rifles were in it!"

CHAPTER III

Telltale Tracks

THE Hardys learned that Chet had gone to the railroad station in the farm truck to pick up a box of high-powered rifles. The guns had been purchased by Tyler Morton, Chet's uncle and famous big-game hunter.

"Uncle Ty's coming to our place in two weeks to get his stuff for a trip to Africa," Chet explained. "But now his plans will be ruined. His guns are gone!"

"How come? Where was the truck?" Frank asked.

Chet said he had loaded the big box onto the truck and then had driven to the Wells Hardware Store to pick up a chest of tools for his father.

"While I was at the store," Chet continued, "I picked out a lot of camping equipment I knew we would need for our trip." Sheepishly he added, "I picked out a dandy canoe, too."

"Did you pay for all this stuff?" Joe queried.

"No. Charged it. I thought if you didn't like the stuff, I could return it." Chet put his head in his hands and moaned. "If I don't get 'em back, I'll have to pay for 'em all!"

"Pretty tough," Frank remarked. "Then what happened?"

"Everything was loaded into the back of the truck," Chet explained. "I started to drive home. But I was hungry, so I pulled into the Pines, a roadside eating place."

"I only had a couple of three-deckers," the plump youth explained. "When I went outside for the truck, it—it was gone."

"You left the keys in it?" Joe asked, frowning.

"Yes."

"How long ago did this happen?" Frank asked. "Did you notify the police, Chet?"

"No. I came right here."

Chet was so flustered he could not remember the license number of the truck. Frank telephoned Chief Collig what had happened. Then he ran out of the house with Chet and Joe, and took the wheel of the boys' convertible.

"We'll start from the Pines," he said.

There was silence for a few seconds, then Joe asked, "Why did you buy all that camping stuff, Chet?"

"We were talking about a trip, weren't we?"

"Nothing was definite."

"I know," Chet admitted.

When they arrived at the restaurant, Chet showed the boys where the truck had been parked.

"Are these marks in the mud from your tires?" Joe asked.

Chet nodded. "Yes. They're plain enough, because those rear tires were new."

The Hardys easily traced the tracks to the road, when they discovered that the truck had headed north.

Frank continued along the highway for nearly two miles, slowing down at each intersection to see if there were any tire marks along the soft sides of the roadway.

At a dirt crossroad Frank stopped to look at some tire prints on the left. After a careful examination, he shouted:

"I see them! But say, another car followed in the truck's tracks. Wonder if that means anything."

Chet was not listening. "Come on!" he shouted.

They hopped into the car and followed the country road. The double tracks continued for some distance; then the boys saw only one set of tire marks.

"Now what?" Frank asked, perplexed.

Joe jumped out. Reason told him the truck had turned off, but where? There was no side road.

In a moment Joe began tearing at some bushes along the road. His trained eye had noted they were wilting; probably torn up a little while before and piled there as a screen.

"Look!" he shouted, pulling the bushes away.

A lumberman's road, which had not been used for years, forked from the dirt country road. Weeds between the logs clearly showed the two crushed trails that the wheels had made.

"Wait here," said Joe.

He disappeared into the woods, but returned in a couple of minutes.

"I found your truck, Chet," he said.

"Hooray!" Chet shouted. "Gee, that's super! Now Uncle Ty can go to Africa and we can take that camping trip!"

"The truck is empty!"

"Oh, no!" Chet's jaw dropped.

Frank had an idea. "I believe the driver of the other car was a pal of the truck thief. They must have known about this wood road where they could work without being seen."

"And loaded the guns, tools, and camping stuff into the car and drove off," Joe said. "A stolen truck's hard to get rid of, but loot isn't."

"What about the canoe?" Frank asked.

"It could have been fastened to the roof. A lot of cars have ski racks on top, you know," Joe replied.

Chet was distressed. A truck thief was bad enough, but going after two men with rifles in their possession was more than he had bargained for.

"I guess we'd better let the police handle this," he said.

"What! Let those thieves get away now, when we're on their trail!" Joe protested. "I'll back the truck out," he offered, "and then we'll go after 'em!"

With Chet's help he maneuvered the truck onto the dirt road, then trailed Frank and Chet for a mile and a half. During the ride Chet was told about the wallet the Hardys had found.

"Wow!" Chet exclaimed. "Two thousand dollars!"

Frank stopped suddenly. Joe pulled up in the truck right behind him and jumped out.

"Trail end?" he asked.

"No. But the car stopped here," Frank replied. "See these marks?"

"You've got good eyesight to catch that," Joe said.

The Hardys concluded that the loot might have been carried into the woods at this point. Bushes were beaten down here and there, and near the edge of a brook footprints were clearly visible. The boys searched up- and downstream, but no further trace of the thieves could be found.

"No point in going any deeper in the woods," Frank said. "We're only guessing that the stolen stuff is here. Anyway, this is North Woods." He winked at Joe. "You know what that means."

Chet's eyes bulged. "You mean the place where people say they've heard wild dogs?"

"The same." Frank nodded. "And a wild dog can be mean."

"I don't want to meet any of 'em," Chet said.

"Not even to get the stolen stuff back?"

"Let the police find it," Chet advised. "And if they don't . . . Say, you fellows got all that money. How about letting me have some of it to pay for the stolen rifles and everything?"

"Not on your life," Joe replied, laughing. "It doesn't belong to us."

Chet groaned. He realized now that it had been a mistake to order the camping equipment without the Hardys' consent. Too often in his life he had made similar mistakes and had had to pay for them with hard work, to which he was allergic.

The Hardys returned to their car. This time Chet drove the truck. Twenty minutes later they came to the intersecting macadam road, Black Horse Pike, where they lost the trail.

"We'd better report that we found the truck," Frank said as he headed back to Bayport.

A couple of miles farther on they came to a State Police substation. Frank went in. After telling the desk sergeant of the recovery of the truck, he reported that a box of valuable big-game rifles, a set of tools, a canoe, and other camping equipment had been removed from it.

The sergeant, a tall, broad-shouldered man, frowned. "High-powered rifles are dangerous weapons in the hands of criminals," he said. "We'll make a careful search right away."

"Thanks," Frank said and went outside. Then Chet said good-by to the brothers and drove off.

When the Hardys arrived home, they found their friends Biff Hooper and Tony Prito waiting. Biff was a tall, lanky boy whose chief delight was his secondhand jeep. Tony, olive-skinned and dark-eyed, could usually be found on Barmet Bay racing his bright-red motorboat the *Napoli*.

"Hi, fellows!" Joe called out.

"What about our camping trip?" Biff asked. "Made any plans?"

"I think we ought to postpone the long trip we had in mind," Frank said. "Let's go to North Woods this weekend instead." He told about the theft of Mr. Morton's truck and the things in it.

"You mean you want us to search North Woods for the rifles and other stuff?" Tony asked.

"That's right."

"If there's anything to those stories about wild dogs out there, we'd better not take any chances," Biff suggested.

"I don't think there's anything to the rumor," Tony scoffed.

After mapping plans for the weekend trip, Biff

and Tony left. Then Joe telephoned Chet. He whistled in alarm at the thought of going into North Woods.

"Okay, if you don't want to go," said Joe. "But it's your stuff that was stolen. What are you going to tell your uncle?"

"You win." Chet sighed. "I'll go."

After an early supper Joe busied himself getting out their sleeping bags. Frank hurried downtown to the newspaper office. There was a remote chance, he thought, that somebody already had answered the ad about the mysterious wallet.

The clerk on duty, a high school friend who worked there evenings, handed Frank an envelope.

"A stranger left this in your box a few minutes ago."

Frank tore it open eagerly. Then he frowned. The message was brief and mystifying.

Don't give the money to anyone until you hear from me again.

The strange note was signed "Rainy Night."

CHAPTER IV

Followed!

"WHAT did the man look like, Ken?" Frank asked excitedly.

The clerk grinned. "Another Hardy mystery, I'll bet. Well, the fellow was short and dark. Had a slight limp. Wore dark glasses."

Frank suspected the stranger might have worn the glasses as a partial disguise. "Did you notice anything special about them?" he asked.

Ken shook his head, then a second later said, "A piece of the frame was broken off."

"Which eye?"

"Listen, Frank, I'm no detective."

"Think!" Frank insisted. "It's important."

"Okay, teacher. I guess it was the left eye," he said slowly as he tried to remember.

"That's swell. Thanks, Ken. It will help a lot."

"Want me to call the cops if he returns?" the clerk asked.

"I'm sure that won't be necessary. Something tells me that man won't show up here again."

Frank said this loud enough to be heard by several persons standing near the counter. Out of the corner of his eye, he watched for any sign of interest, in case the mysterious fellow with the dark glasses might have a pal posted to watch for the person who had placed the ad. A man who had his back turned seemed to be listening.

"Somebody ought to follow him," Frank thought.

Moving quietly to a telephone booth at one end of the office, he dialed his home. Joe answered.

"Frank, what's up?"

"I'm at the *News* office. A strange note was left for us. I think that the man who wrote it or a pal of his may try to follow me. Come down and watch, will you?"

"Right."

Frank stepped from the booth and resumed his conversation with his friend Ken. A few minutes later he saw Joe walk past the door. Shortly afterward, Frank said good night to the clerk and ambled out.

A woman who had been thumbing through some back issues in the newspaper file immediately started after Frank. She wore a hat which shaded her face most effectively, so that Frank could not distinguish her features.

Frank lingered a moment in front of the building to look at some photographs in the display window. The woman crossed the street and went into a store.

As Frank started on, a tall, blond-haired man, intently reading a newspaper which partially concealed his face, emerged from the store.

Frank saw Joe's reflection in a store window across the street. Joe was following him at a discreet distance. Frank tried to act as though he was unhurried. The man, looking up from his newspaper, but keeping his face turned as if still looking in the shopwindows, followed at the same gait.

Frank walked faster. So did the man. A few moments later Frank looked back. To his dismay, he saw that the woman was now following Joe!

Frank turned from South Street into Market Street. Glancing over his shoulder a few seconds later, he noticed that no one else had rounded the corner. He retraced his steps, gazing here and there on the sidewalk as if he had dropped something. Joe, the man, and the woman had vanished.

Frank peered down side streets and through open doorways. There was no sign of any of them. He was just beginning to feel worried, when far down the block he saw Joe wave at him.

Frank halted while Joe caught up. "Where'd they go?" Frank asked. "And where have you been?"

"Chasing 'em."

Joe reported that he had heard a whistle behind

him. Turning, he had seen the woman. Both she and the man had ducked into a service driveway and disappeared.

"Sure seems as if they're working together," Frank commented. "I wonder if they've stopped following us."

"Let's hope so," said Joe. "Too bad I didn't get a good look at that man's face."

His brother nodded. "If those people are after the two thousand dollars we found, they'll try something else to learn who has it."

"Maybe I was dumb to signal you," Joe said. "That man and woman probably are watching us right now."

The Hardys decided to separate and take zigzag routes home to throw any possible pursuers off the track. Fifteen minutes later they reached the house. For nearly an hour they discussed the affair with their mother and aunt.

"It's a good thing you shook those brassy creatures," Aunt Gertrude declared. "Why, they might have murdered us all in our beds! And to no avail, either, with the money locked up at police headquarters."

Next morning, as the boys were eating breakfast, Aunt Gertrude, who had been out for an early-morning walk, bustled into the house.

"Look at this!" she cried. "I found these glasses under the porch window. They don't belong to us. Somebody must have been looking in and dropped them. Somebody has been spying on our house!"

"The man at the newspaper office!" Joe exclaimed.

"Let's see 'em," Frank asked.

A piece had been broken out of the left side of the frame!

"Our man, all right, Joe," he said. "We *were* followed, sure enough. Aunt Gertrude, what window was he looking in?"

She led the way to the far window on the porch which opened into the living room. Both boys began an examination of the spot. Finding no visible clues, Joe went for a magnifying glass. With it he spotted fresh fingerprints on the window sill.

"We'd better photograph these pronto," he said, and went to the boys' laboratory for the equipment.

Mr. Hardy had taught his sons the latest method of using powder, camera, and developers. In a few minutes the fingerprints of the mysterious prowler were recorded. Frank and Joe hurried to Chief Collig with them. They told the chief of their adventure of the evening before and requested that the prints be checked out.

The result was disappointing. The fingerprints did not belong to any wanted well-known criminal, nor to any local person with a police record.

"I'll send these prints along to the FBI in Washington if you want me to," Collig said.

"No, thanks," said Frank. "We'll wait till Dad comes back."

Upon reaching home, the boys looked for matching fingerprints on the frames of the glasses. But unfortunately the only clear ones were Aunt Gertrude's. The glasses were placed on a shelf in the laboratory marked *Visible Evidence*.

On their way to the second floor the boys met their mother on the stairway. "Do you suppose that snooper will come again?" she asked anxiously. "Oh dear! I wish your father were home!"

"Don't worry, Mother," Frank said quickly. "I think the fellow wanted to find out if we had the money at home. He probably overheard us talking and learned it's at police headquarters."

That afternoon Frank and Joe dropped into the *News* office for more mail. In all, they were handed four letters. None had any bearing on their case. Each one named a smaller sum of money and obviously referred to some other loss.

"Well, we haven't found the owner of the two thousand yet," Frank said. "Now I'm convinced."

"Of what?"

"The money really was stolen. That's why the person who lost it won't openly claim it."

"I'll bet you're right, Frank," his brother said. "So we can expect more trouble."

"Exactly."

They agreed not to mention their concern to Mrs. Hardy or Aunt Gertrude. There was no need of frightening them. During the leisurely evening meal they discussed various other matters, including the night ball game they planned to attend, also the trip to North Woods.

"How is Callie?" Mrs. Hardy asked, smiling at Frank, who was taking the girl to the game. Her son thought that Callie Shaw was the nicest girl at Bayport High.

"All right, I guess," he answered. "I haven't talked to her since yesterday."

"Tsk, tsk!" Joe spoke up. "Such neglect!"

"Cut it," Frank begged. "And you'd better get busy soon, Joe, or Iola will go with someone else."

Joe glanced at the clock. He barely had time to drive out to the Morton farm to pick up Chet's sister Iola. Excusing himself, he left the table.

"See you at the ball park in three-quarters of an hour, Frank," he called.

Frank set off on foot thirty minutes later. Callie's house was only a few blocks from the Hardy home and was on the way to the ball field. The sun had set, and a cool evening breeze stirred the leaves of the big trees which shaded the avenue.

The boy was deep in thought about the mystery which he and Joe had stumbled upon. Would they hear again from the letterwriter who signed himself Rainy Night?

Reaching a wooded section where the houses were far apart, he heard a slight rustle behind a hedge. Almost immediately, a dark figure came hurtling over the evergreen hedge. Before Frank could dodge, the man flung himself upon him in a diving tackle.

Frank was blindfolded and gagged before he could attempt to defend himself or cry out. His head was still spinning when he became aware of another man on the scene.

"You got him, eh? Good!"

"What now?" asked the second man.

"Into the car."

Four hands dragged Frank along the ground and heaved him onto the floor in the rear of a sedan!

CHAPTER V

The Ransom Demand

JOE HARDY, meanwhile, drove happily along the highway toward the Morton farm. The prospect of a good ball game pleased him, especially since he was to see it with Iola. Iola was as slim as her brother was chubby, but she had the same kind of tilted nose and twinkling eyes. Glossy black hair fell softly to her shoulders.

It was not long before Joe drew up to the Morton home. Iola and Chet came out to meet him.

"Ready for some grand-slam homers?" Joe asked.

"I'll settle for a couple of triple plays," Iola replied, dimpling.

"Let's go," Joe said. "We'll save you a seat, Chet. Frank's taking Callie."

Soon they were on the outskirts of the ball field. Joe parked the car, bought two tickets, and found seats.

"I thought Frank and Callie would be here by this time," Joe said, looking around. "We'll hold three seats as long as we can."

The Oakmont Blues trotted onto the field for their warmup. After they had batted a few times and chased a few fungoes, the Bayport Bears replaced them on the diamond.

"I don't like this," Joe said, beginning to feel uneasy.

Iola touched his arm. "Don't worry," she said. "Maybe they wanted to sit by themselves."

Joe knew Frank would not do this without telling him. He kept surveying the faces of new arrivals. Finally he spotted Chet and waved him over to where they were sitting.

"Hiya, kids!" Chet bubbled. "Glad you saved a seat for me. Say, where are the others?"

"They haven't arrived," Joe said.

He tried not to appear anxious, but the strange happenings of the past two days made him apprehensive. Joe could not keep his mind on the game.

"I'm going to phone and see if I can find out what happened to Frank and Callie," he said. "Iola, you wait here with Chet."

He hurried to a telephone booth at the rear of the ball park and dialed the Shaw home. Callie answered.

"Is Frank there?"

"No, Joe. And I haven't heard from him. Has something happened?"

"I hope not," Joe replied tersely. "Callie, I can't understand this. Will you stay where you are until you hear from me again?"

The gasp on the other end of the line told Joe that Callie's concern was as deep as his own.

"I'll let you know as soon as I find out anything," Joe promised.

He hung up and then quickly telephoned his home. Aunt Gertrude said Frank had left the house thirty minutes after Joe.

Joe went for the boys' car and drove to Callie's house. From there he walked over the route, now dark, which he thought Frank would have taken, but reached home without finding his brother.

"I'll get a flashlight and look again," Joe said to himself as he unlocked the front door.

Mrs. Hardy and Aunt Gertrude were startled to see Joe and immediately shared his worries.

"We'll all look," said Mrs. Hardy.

Aunt Gertrude grabbed a hickory cane from the hall closet. "I'll beat the daylights out of anyone who has laid a hand on Frank!" she vowed.

The three hurried from the house and walked slowly along the street to Callie's. Joe led the way, flashing his light from side to side. When they reached the wooded section, Joe bent down. Signs of a struggle were apparent to his trained eyes. Then he saw something that sent a spasm of fear to the pit of his stomach.

Frank's initialed handkerchief!

There was no doubt now that somebody had ambushed Frank.

Two lines that looked as though they had been made by dragging shoe heels led to the curb. The flashlight revealed oil stains in the street indicating that a car had stood in the lonely spot for some time before being driven off.

Mrs. Hardy began to tremble. "Oh, my boy, my boy!" she said. "How can we find him?"

Aunt Gertrude kept her emotions under control. "We'll go home and get the police busy at once. Joe, you run ahead and phone them."

The boy reached the Hardy house just as a tall, distinguished-looking man was striding up the front walk. In one hand he carried a traveling bag, in the other a bulging briefcase.

"Dad!"

Mr. Hardy turned to greet his son. His keen dark eyes caught the look of alarm in Joe's face.

"Dad, we're afraid Frank's been kidnapped!"

"Easy, son. Come inside and give me all the facts."

Joe was telling his father of the recent mysterious happenings when his mother and aunt came hurrying into the living room. Greetings were brief and Mrs. Hardy became calmer now that her husband was home. Joe continued his story. The detective paced the floor as he listened, while Mrs. Hardy and Aunt Gertrude sat by, their faces reflecting their anxiety.

As Joe finished, there was a rap on the door. In rushed Chet and Iola.

"Where's Frank?" Iola cried. "I just couldn't watch the game any longer. We phoned Callie. I . . ."

The telephone rang. Mr. Hardy picked it up.

"Hello. Fenton Hardy speaking."

"This is Rainy Night. We have your son, Hardy," a man's steely voice came over the wire. "Send us ten thousand dollars in fifty-dollar bills if you want him back alive."

Though alarmed, the detective's jaw tensed with anger. His voice was razor-sharp as he answered, "Whoever you are, I want to remind you that there's a law against kidnapping."

"Keep the police out of this," came the cool reply.

"Release that boy immediately," Mr. Hardy said as everybody in the room stood electrified.

"Not till you pay!"

Mr. Hardy, though exasperated, was worried. His bluff had not worked. "Where shall we pay you the money?"

"You'll know in the morning. Have the cash ready by eight-thirty." The receiver clicked.

Then Mr. Hardy told his wife and son that the man on the wire had demanded a ransom for the delivery of Frank.

"Don't any of you mention this until I give the

"Who sent these?" Joe asked in surprise

word," Mr. Hardy warned. "It may mean Frank's life if we're not careful."

In trembling anxiety Chet and Iola went home, pledged to keep the secret. Then Joe telephoned to Callie, telling her not to worry, and saying he would pick up his car in the morning.

Sleep came fitfully to all in the Hardy household. In the morning they showed the strain of a night of anguish.

While they were listlessly eating breakfast, the doorbell rang. It was exactly eight o'clock. Joe rushed to answer. An expressman stood on the porch, holding a cage partially wrapped in burlap and containing two pigeons.

"Who sent these?" Joe asked in surprise.

The man glanced at the label. "Gemini Bird's his name."

"What a phony!" Joe exclaimed. "That means twin bird!"

Joe signed for the birds and carried the cage into the living room. The other Hardys rushed from the dining room.

"What in creation!" Aunt Gertrude exclaimed.

Mrs. Hardy looked at her husband for an explanation. "So this is the way the ransom money is to be delivered," the detective said.

Joe looked at the pigeons' legs. "They're not banded," he remarked. "Homing pigeons are usually numbered, aren't they, Dad?"

"Yes. A very clever person is behind this move," Mr. Hardy said grimly. "These pigeons will fly straight to the culprits who kidnapped Frank, and we'll never find out who they are. But," the detective added with set jaw, "I'll find a way to trap them!"

CHAPTER VI

Tailing a Pigeon

CONSCIOUSNESS rushed back into Frank's brain. He was aware of a distant bell tolling eight o'clock. Was it morning or evening? He could see nothing because of the blindfold fastened tightly around his head.

The boy's ankles were tied, his wrists bound behind him, and the gag still was in his mouth. Now memory returned. After he had been attacked and thrown into the car, a gruff voice had said:

"Easy now. This kid's worth ten grand." A long ride had followed. The car had stopped and the boy had been carried into a house.

The last words he had heard were, "That should hold him over!" A needle had punctured his arm. Then he had blacked out.

How long he had lain in the darkness Frank did not know. His whole body ached from the tight cords with which his wrists and ankles were bound. What day was it? he wondered.

With every ounce of effort, Frank rolled over and over on the earthen floor until he hit a wall. Rubbing his head against it, he was able to slip off the blindfold. By the daylight coming through a dirty window high above him, Frank realized he was in a cellar.

On the floor near him lay a piece of broken pipe. Frank wriggled across the dirty cellar floor. After a great deal of painful maneuvering he was able to bring his wrist bonds in contact with the jagged edge of the broken drainpipe.

The pipe rolled away, and the boy had to wedge it between the floor and the wall before he could saw the rope back and forth across the rusty edge of the pipe. The effort was painful and exhausting. But at last the rope parted and his hands were free. Quickly he loosened his gag and untied the rope that bound his ankles. He rose and walked around to stretch his cramped muscles.

The house was silent. Were the thugs upstairs, ready to deal with him further?

There was no door leading to the outside, so Frank noiselessly lifted the window, fastening it with a rusty hook. He sprang upward, at the same time thrusting his head out the window and putting his weight on his elbows. Nobody was in sight.

Digging his toes against the side of the cellar wall, Frank cautiously wormed his way through the low window. Weather-beaten shutters hung grotesquely from what obviously was a farmhouse, and the front door stood open on a broken hinge. The place seemed to be deserted.

Frank looked around and tried to get his bearings. To the north was a wooded mountain with a dip in the peak. Recognizing the mountaintop formation, he decided that the farm must be located on the same road off which they had found Chet's abandoned truck—only farther from town.

"Those birds must know this territory well," he thought.

Remembering another farmhouse a mile or so in the direction of Black Horse Pike, Frank set off. He was faint from hunger and the drug, but he kept on. As he plodded up the lane, the farmer's wife saw him coming and opened the door. She surveyed the disheveled boy skeptically.

"May I use your telephone?" he asked. "I'm Frank Hardy, and I want to call Bayport."

On hearing the name Hardy, the woman readily consented. Frank put his call through. As he waited, he noticed that the hands on a mantel clock stood at eight twenty-five.

Mr. Hardy answered. "Frank? . . . Is this you? . . . Hold the wire a second." His voice boomed into the distance, "Don't let that pigeon go!"

Frank was perplexed. He could hear sounds of the detective returning to the telephone.

"Are you all right, Frank?" Mr. Hardy asked.

"I'm fine, Dad," Frank replied. "I got away. Will you pick me up on Black Horse Pike? I'll walk there. I'm calling from a farm on the North Woods road."

Joe was listening, too. "We'll burn up the tires!" he shouted.

Frank hung up, thanked the woman, and paid her for the call. She insisted that he sit down in the kitchen and have some rolls and milk, which he accepted gratefully. His feeling of weakness and dizziness was rapidly disappearing.

"Is that old farmhouse down the road deserted?" he asked, pointing in the direction where he had spent the night.

"Yes, 'tis," she replied. "The old folks passed away and nobody wants the place."

"Anybody been using it since they left?" Frank asked casually.

The woman laughed. "That tumble-down place? Who'd want to stay there?"

"Tramps might—or somebody looking for a hideout."

The farm woman bristled. "Young man, we don't tolerate no folks like that in this peace-abiding neighborhood!"

Frank could have pointed out the error in her contention, but he said nothing. Thanking her for her hospitality, he departed. He walked down the dirt road to Black Horse Pike, where he sat down and waited to be picked up.

When Mr. Hardy and Joe arrived in the detective's car, there was an enthusiastic exchange of greetings, then a quick ride back to the Hardy home. On the way, Frank was told about the ransom demand and the crate of pigeons that had arrived that morning.

"I was just going to release one of the pigeons when you phoned," Mr. Hardy said.

The boys' mother and Aunt Gertrude were overjoyed to see Frank safely home once more. They listened spellbound as he related all that had happened.

"I wonder why they left you unguarded," Joe said.

"They probably thought the hypo would make me sleep longer than I did."

"Those men may return again," Mr. Hardy remarked. "We'll notify the police to post a guard at the old farmhouse." He reached for the telephone.

"And a guard for this house, too," Aunt Gertrude demanded.

It was midday when they received a return call from the police saying that the deserted house had been watched constantly but that nobody had come there yet.

"Dad," said Frank, "what would you think of our releasing one of the pigeons and following it to the kidnappers' hideout?"

"You must have been reading my mind, son.

Call the airport and charter a plane. Joe, you get our binoculars."

The detective and his sons set off for the airport with one of the pigeons in the cage. They were greeted at the Ace Air Service by a young pilot named Jack Wayne.

"Where would you like me to take you?" he asked genially.

"That depends upon this pigeon," Mr. Hardy answered, and quickly explained their plan.

"I've chased the enemy many a time." The pilot laughed. "But this is my first time chasing a bird!"

"We'll let the pigeon out at a thousand feet," Mr. Hardy said.

When they reached that altitude, Joe released the bird. It flew away from the plane and began circling to orient itself.

The pilot kept right behind the bird, flying the craft round and round in ever-widening circles.

Joe kept his binoculars trained on the pigeon. Finally the bird got its beam and flew straight toward the south.

After an hour of steady flying, the pilot turned to Mr. Hardy. "How far do you want to follow it, sir?"

"Until your fuel's low."

The detective and his sons conferred on the situation. There was no telling how far the pigeon would fly. The fuel supply of the plane might be exhausted long before the bird alighted.

"One thing is certain," Frank said. "The thugs who kidnapped me have pals in some other part of the country."

Twenty minutes later the pilot said he would have to return to the airport because someone else had chartered a flight.

After they had returned to Bayport and paid the pilot, the Hardys drove home, disappointed that their mission had been fruitless.

"Dad, what is this new case you are working on in Washington?" Joe asked presently. "Can you let us in on it?"

Mr. Hardy looked searchingly at his sons. "It's a top-secret assignment," he said, "but I know I can trust you to keep it."

With rapt attention, Frank and Joe listened while the famous detective unfolded a tale of foreign intrigue. United States currency was being stolen in various Central and South American countries. It was suspected the money was being used to carry out some nefarious schemes. What these were had not yet been discovered.

"I'm working with the FBI on the United States end of the case," Mr. Hardy said. "Other investigators are operating in the foreign countries."

"Sounds exciting," Joe commented. "You have no idea what the thieves are using the money for?"

"Not yet. But we think it is being spent in the United States."

"Is the money being smuggled in across the border?" Frank asked.

"We don't know yet."

"It could be by boat or plane, then?"

"Yes."

Frank and Joe looked at each other. Had their find of two thousand dollars anything to do with their father's case?

CHAPTER VII

A Suspicious Salesman

"Dad, could it be possible we're working on the same case?" Joe asked.

"I'll know better when I see the bills you found. I have the serial numbers of some of the stolen money."

"The two thousand is at police headquarters," Frank said. "Let's go there now."

Frank drove the car and stopped at Bayport Police Headquarters. The Hardys went in.

"I'm glad you got away from those thugs," Chief Collig said to Frank.

"So am I." The youth grinned, then sobered. "Any news of Chet Morton's stolen stuff?"

The chief said he was sorry to report that there was not a trace of it so far. "But I'm certain it's not in Bayport," he added quickly.

Frank and Joe were not so sure.

"If the loot's out in the country, the State Police will probably find it soon," Collig assured them.

"I hope so," said Frank, and explained the reason for their call.

Collig opened the safe and took out the wallet, which he placed on a table. Mr. Hardy withdrew the bills and very slowly began to count them aloud. Frank noticed his father's eyes scanning the printing as he flipped the bills over.

"That's two thousand, all right," the detective remarked. He handed it back to the chief.

"I could have told you that," Collig said with a frown. He had expected more than this from the great detective.

Mr. Hardy thanked the officer for his cooperation, then he and his sons returned to their car.

"Find out anything?" Joe asked eagerly.

"Yes. One of those hundred-dollar bills had a serial number we're looking for! We three are in this together," Mr. Hardy said with a smile of satisfaction.

"Couldn't be better!" Joe shouted enthusiastically. "Look out, Rainy Night, here come the Hardys!"

When they reached home, Aunt Gertrude was reading the evening *News* on the front porch.

"Look at this!" she cried out, waving the newspaper in front of them. " 'Hardy Boy Captured,

Released by Thugs.' Why do newspapers get everything mixed up? Frank got away by himself! I'll write to that editor!"

The boys were amused as well as pleased at their aunt's loyalty. Even though she objected to their working on mystery cases, she was always secretly proud of their exploits and wanted no one else to be given any credit for their achievements.

The story went on to say that Frank was safe and that the authorities were looking for the kidnappers.

"Just the same," Mrs. Hardy spoke up, "I'd feel better if those awful men didn't know where Frank and Joe are."

"You have a good point," her husband agreed. "Boys, why not go on that camping trip you were talking about?"

His sons grinned. "We planned to go to North Woods this weekend and hunt for Chet's stolen stuff."

"Excellent idea," his father said. "Combine work with pleasure."

"North Woods," Aunt Gertrude snorted, "is full of wild dogs! You boys must be out of your minds."

"The stories about the dogs are only rumors," Frank reminded her.

Mr. Hardy suggested it was possible someone had started the rumor to keep intruders away from the area. He warned his sons to be on guard.

The boys' mother announced a new worry. Her sons might be followed into the wilderness by the kidnappers.

"Why not try leaving here without letting anyone see you?" she suggested. "Stay at Chet's house tonight and start from there in the early morning."

Frank and Joe liked their mother's plan. They telephoned Chet, and also Biff Hooper and Tony Prito. The latter two promised to meet them at the Morton farm right after breakfast.

"Chet sure sounded low," Frank commented. "I guess his dad and uncle were pretty sore when they heard what happened."

"Iola told me he's got to work on the farm all summer long to pay for the stuff if it's not found," Joe said.

Frank chuckled. "That'll take off the pounds."

Frank and Joe packed their equipment in the trunk of Mr. Hardy's car. After dark they got in and lay on the floor of the rear seat, then their father drove to the Mortons'. The boys did not show their heads until they were at the farm.

"If anybody is looking for us, they won't know whether we've left the house or not," Joe remarked.

They unloaded the gear and the detective turned the car around. Wishing his sons good luck, he said he was going to Washington for further checking on the stolen-currency case.

After a hearty breakfast the next morning, Chet, Frank, and Joe went out on the porch to wait for Biff and Tony. They had been sitting there only a few minutes when they saw a man, carrying a bulging bag, coming up the driveway. He was fairly tall, had light-colored hair, and shrewd-looking eyes.

"I'm selling insect repellent," the stranger began. "The most wonderful stuff in the world. Use it on the farm or anywhere. Kills flies, moths, mosquitoes."

Chet became interested. "We could use some of that for our camping trip."

The man smiled. "Camping trip, eh? Then you'll want a lot of my repellent. Plenty of flies in the woods. Where you going?"

"To North . . ."

Joe's elbow jabbed into his friend's ribs. Chet was telling the stranger too much!

"North—uh—uh—North Carolina. That is, someday," Chet stammered.

"How much do you want?" the salesman asked.

"None, I guess," Chet replied glumly, embarrassed about the blunder he had made.

"As you please," the man said.

He picked up his bag and walked down the drive. As he shuffled off toward the next farmhouse, Joe grasped Frank's arm.

"I don't like this," he said. "If that man were a real salesman, he would have given us a high-pressure sales talk."

"You're right. He might have been the one who followed me from the *News* office. He's about the same size and blond. That man was sent here to learn something. We'll have to be mighty careful on our trip."

"I'm only sorry Chet practically told him where we are going," Joe declared.

In a few minutes Biff Hooper and Tony Prito arrived.

The boys were told about the new developments in the mystery and the recent episode of the pseudosalesman.

"I've a hunch we'll see him again," Joe said. "He may even follow us to North Woods."

"We'll be ready for him," Tony vowed.

After piling their camping equipment in Chet's car, the boys climbed in. The jalopy snorted and started off down the road.

When they neared the North Woods area, Frank said, "Let's park at the farmhouse where I made the telephone call. Then we can start the hike to the woods from there."

This agreed upon, Chet turned onto the lonely dirt road. When they arrived at the farmhouse, the woman gladly let them leave the car behind the barn. The boys took out their gear and after a cold drink of water at the pump started their trek toward North Woods.

As they passed the deserted house where Frank had been held captive, the boy's spine tingled. Had the thugs planned to leave him there to die, he wondered. Or would they have freed him after the ransom had been collected?

The campers walked another mile, then headed into the woods at the point where they thought Chet's stolen stuff might have been carried in. Upon reaching the brook where the suspect's footprints had ended, they stopped to confer on which way to proceed. The trees and underbrush stretched for miles, wild and apparently uninhabited.

"Well, you detectives," Tony said, "where in this jungle did that thief go?"

Frank was sure they would have taken the path of least resistance into the forest. After all, the canoe would be an unwieldy thing to carry in dense woodland.

"Okay," Tony said with a grin. "You find it."

The boys resumed the trek, with Frank and Joe in the lead. After they had pressed forward for an hour, Chet stopped and flung his pack to the ground. "Say, fellows, do you know where you're going?" he puffed.

"Sure," said Frank. "In the direction the thieves took."

"How do you know?"

"By this." Frank had just spotted what might be a clue.

He bent down beside a rough rock, twice the size of a man's head. Somebody apparently had stepped on it and slipped, making a deep heel impression in the moss beside it.

Frank whipped a magnifying glass from his pack and examined the rock. It revealed minute shreds of leather where the uneven surface of the boulder had abraded the shoe.

"I think we're on the right track," he said. "Come on, Chet."

An hour later the boys stopped for lunch. Then after a rest they moved on again, following a mountain stream. They were on the alert the rest of the afternoon, but found no further evidence that the thieves had preceded them. More than once the Hardys had to reassure their friends that they were on the right track. It was the only half-way open route by which heavily laden men could have penetrated the densely forested area.

Finally they decided to make camp. Tony prepared a satisfying hot meal of beans and bacon.

As the boys ate it, Chet gave a huge sigh. "I'm afraid that stolen stuff's gone forever." he said. "Listen, fellows, you haven't any plans for the summer. How about giving me a hand at the farm to help pay for it?"

"Never milked a cow in my life," was Tony's excuse.

"Pitching hay makes me sneeze something awful," said Biff. He shifted his long legs and yawned.

"Doctor says bouncing on a tractor is bad for my heart," Joe piped up.

Chet refused to laugh. "Then you simply got to find that stuff!" he declared.

"We?" Frank chortled. "We're only helping you."

Chet grunted, took an extra helping of beans, and announced he was hitting the sack early. All the boys, tired from their long trek, crawled into their sleeping bags within half an hour after eating.

In the middle of the night the campers awoke suddenly. Some noise had aroused them. They listened. In the distance an animal howled.

But there had been another sound, too.

A wailing siren!

CHAPTER VIII

The Night Prowler

THE campers sat bolt upright as the siren wailed again, its mournful tone fading in the distance.

"That's the same sound we heard over the ocean, Joe!" Frank said in a hoarse whisper.

Instinctively both boys had looked up, associating the sound with a helicopter. But there was no aircraft overhead.

"Hey, what's up?" Chet called.

The boys listened, but the mysterious wailing sound was not repeated.

"You're sure it was the same sound you heard just before you found the money?" Biff asked.

"It sure was," Joe declared.

Propped on their elbows, the five boys speculated about the source of the noise and what might happen next. Suddenly the howling of the animal they had heard a few minutes before began again. It seemed to be nearer now.

"It's a wild dog!" Chet cried out. "He's smelled us. He might bring his whole pack here!"

Biff suggested building a fire to frighten off the animal.

"But that'll focus attention on us," Frank objected. "If the siren has anything to do with the money, my kidnappers might spot us."

The others agreed and waited in the dark. Presently the howling animal became quiet, so the boys settled themselves once more in their sleeping bags.

The next morning while having breakfast, they talked about the disturbance of the previous night.

"Say, it's eight o'clock," Biff interrupted, glancing at his watch. "Think I'll listen to the news. We might learn something that will explain that siren."

He reached into his pack, drew out a transistor radio, and tuned in the Bayport station. The voice of the announcer was excited, telling of the disappearance of a plane. The pilot, Jack Wayne, had taken off from Bayport the night before. A short time later he had contacted the airport by radio.

"I'm in trouble!" he had cried. "Hijackers!" Nothing more had been heard from him.

"It's thought he may have crashed on the ocean or in the woodlands beyond Bayport," the announcer said. "The Coast Guard has been alerted, and State Police have started a search."

The Hardys looked at each other, dismayed. Jack Wayne! The pilot who had taken them up only the day before yesterday.

"If Wayne came down in these woods," Frank said soberly, "I'm afraid he's in bad shape."

The campers decided to combine looking for him with hunting for the articles stolen from the Morton truck. They listened to the rest of the broadcast while packing up, but there was no other news of particular interest to the boys.

Frank and Joe suggested that they proceed in the direction from which the siren sound had come, and the five set off. As they scrambled along through the dense thickets, the boys talked about the disturbing broadcast.

"A stowaway might have knocked Wayne out," Frank suggested. "But you've given me an idea, Chet. Maybe Wayne didn't crash. He may have been kidnapped!"

Nevertheless, all the boys watched for signs of an accident as they pressed deeper into the pathless woodland. Talk ceased when they began ascending a rugged slope. Perspiration drenched the shirts of the hikers by the time they reached the ridge. Chet was puffing, and his face was as red as a beet.

"Let's rest here awhile, fellows, and look over the valley," he suggested.

"Maybe we can spot something if we climb one of the trees," said Tony.

He walked toward an old fir, which towered like a sentinel.

"Stand on my shoulders and catch the first branch," Biff offered.

He leaned over to help him, and Tony soon was on his way up the tree. When he reached the top he shaded his eyes with one hand.

"Swell view," he called. "I can see all the way to the bay."

"Any sign of Jack's plane?" Joe called up.

"Or of the thieves who stole my stuff?" Chet shouted.

The reply was negative to both questions, but Tony continued to gaze around him in every direction. Suddenly he cried out:

"I see something shiny way off there." He pointed deeper into the forest. "Maybe it's part of the lost plane."

The youth climbed down and led the way over swampy ground and through a tangle of tamaracks in the direction of the gleaming object. After an hour's hike, he said:

"I guess I've found it. It's not a plane. It's a pond."

The boys followed Tony through a clump of thick brush. Beyond it in the sun lay a good-sized body of water.

"Oh, brother," exclaimed Chet, "could I use a swim right now!"

The other boys agreed and stripped off their clothes.

"Race you across the pond, Frank," Joe called, taking a shallow dive.

He beat his brother to the far side by only one length. They pulled up on the bank and sat down.

Frank, looking about him, noticed the remains of a campfire nearby. He got up and walked over to it. There were several backbones of fish. Someone had cooked and eaten there recently!

"I wonder if it was one of the gang we're after," he said excitedly. "Say, here are some good footprints!"

The young detectives tried to follow them, but the going was too painful on their bare feet.

"Let's come back when we have shoes on," Joe suggested.

They swam back to the other shore and reported their discovery.

"Now we're getting somewhere," said Chet. "But gosh, I'm awful tired. Can't we wait awhile before we chase that guy?"

The Hardys offered to follow the trail of the footprints while the others did some fishing. Immediately after lunch Joe and Frank resumed their search for the unknown fisherman. His marks were plainly visible in the soft ground near the pond, but as soon as the earth grew hard, they ended.

"Let's continue in the same direction," Frank suggested. "The fellow may have a cabin up ahead."

They went on for a quarter of a mile but found nothing, and decided that the man must have changed his course. Frank thought it might be a good idea for all of the campers to remain in the vicinity of the pond for a while.

"That man will probably come back," he added.

The Hardys rejoined their friends. At sunset they moved camp across the pond, out of sight of the stranger's old campfire.

The boys enjoyed Tony's catch of sunfish, then listened to the radio. There was no word of the missing Jack Wayne, the newscaster said. Presently Chet began to yawn loudly, and all decided that it was time to turn in.

"Don't sleep too soundly," Frank told his brother. "Keep one eye open for visitors."

Joe nodded. It was not long before the heavy breathing of the other three boys blended with the sounds of the woodland night. Frank and Joe dozed fitfully. An hour later Frank leaned over and nudged his brother.

"I'm sure I heard footsteps," he whispered, looking around. "There they are again!"

A slight sound of crackling underbrush came to their ears. Suddenly a light flashed. It was trained directly on the Hardy boys.

"Who are you?" Frank shouted, leaping out of his bag and arousing the entire camp.

There was no answer. The light went out and retreating footsteps hurried off in the underbrush.

Frank put on his shoes, grabbed his flashlight, and darted after the intruder.

"Chet, Biff, Tony, watch camp! There may be others! Come on, Joe!" he shouted.

One thing was certain. The stranger knew his way in the dark. Soon he was so far ahead of the boys that they could no longer hear his sprinting footsteps.

"I hate to give up," Frank said in disgust. "But we'd never find him now."

They turned back, wondering if the intruder had been one of the thieves they were after, or only some hermit who did not want his hideout to be discovered.

Upon reaching camp, they found the others excited and worried. Biff had picked up a note the mysterious caller had dropped. It was evident that the purpose of his visit had been to leave a warning. The piece of dirty paper bore a message written in pencil:

Get out of these woods. You're in danger.

"Maybe we ought to leave," Chet said.

The Hardys were convinced that the warning note proved that a person or persons in North Woods did not want the boys around. Unless the writer had something to hide, why would he ob-ject to their presence?

"We'll stay," said Frank.

"Let's set up watches," Joe suggested.

Since it was already one o'clock, each was as-signed to an hour's sentry duty. However, the rest of the night passed without incident.

At six they all arose. Frank, who had been on watch the past hour, said he had discovered a nar-row, clear stream near the pond.

"Good drinking water," he said.

Chet was sent off with the canteens while the others prepared breakfast. He had been gone only a few minutes when he let out a war whoop.

The boys dashed in the direction from which Chet's shout had come. Chet was leaning far over an undercut in the bank, tugging at something which they could not see.

The stout boy turned his head and motioned. "Come here quick! I've found the stolen canoe!"

CHAPTER IX

A Cry for Help

IN the tiny lagoon, almost hidden by the eelgrass at the water's edge, floated a canoe.

"Are you sure it's the same canoe?" Joe asked.

Chet pointed to a deep nick in the varnished wood, saying Wells Hardware had knocked something off the original price because of the imperfection.

"Maybe the other stolen stuff isn't far away," Joe said enthusiastically.

"You mean the thief hid the canoe here?" Chet asked.

"It might have drifted down the river," Joe suggested. "There aren't any paddles in it."

"Let's go up the river after breakfast and take a look," said Frank.

The Hardys fashioned two crude paddles. While Biff and Tony remained to watch the camp, the other three started up the river. Joe kneeled in the bow and Frank in the stern. Chet sat down in the middle facing Frank.

"Joe, you watch the left bank for signs of the thief," Frank suggested as his crude paddle dipped into the shallow, rock-filled water. "I'll take the right."

"What about me?" Chet queried. "Don't I look anywhere?"

"You're ballast," Joe needled. "All you do is sit tight."

But Frank was more serious. "Watch the rear, Chet. See if anybody steps out of hiding after we go past."

The three boys proceeded slowly upstream. All eyes strained for a glimpse of a human being, a hut, or any other place where the stolen rifles, tools, and camp equipment might be hidden.

For a long time there was silence except for the gurgling of the ripples around the rocks and the dipping of the paddles.

Then Joe let out a whistle. He indicated a lean-to near the riverbank.

"Let's investigate it," he said, resting his paddle.

They landed and Chet held onto the canoe while Frank and Joe looked in the lean-to. A pair of hiking boots stood in one corner.

"They're new," Frank remarked as he examined them. "Say, here's a long scratch." The shiny leather on the right one had been deeply marred.

"The fellow who slipped on the rock in the woods!" Joe guessed. "I wonder where he is."

"One of us ought to hide here to see who comes for the shoes," said Frank. "Suppose we all paddle off, so if he's around here now, he won't be suspicious. One of us can sneak back through the woods."

Joe volunteered. At a bend in the river, he hopped ashore and carefully retraced his way to the lean-to.

Five, ten, fifteen minutes went by. Merely sitting and waiting behind a large tree began to irk the restless boy. He decided to do a little scouting.

"But which way?" he wondered.

While Joe stood trying to decide, his nostrils caught the scent of wood smoke. He knew he was too far from the boys' camp for smoke to be detected. Turning slowly and sniffing the air at intervals, he finally concluded it was coming from a direction at right angles to the river.

Keeping an alert watch for anything suspicious, Joe headed inland. The scent grew stronger. It was not long before he came to a small clearing, in the center of which smoldered a campfire. Nobody was in sight.

The young detective remained in concealment a few minutes. Then he examined the ashes. The heat they still radiated was mute evidence that somebody had been there within the past few minutes. Was he the person who used the lean-to?

"Maybe he went back there," Joe thought. "I'd better find out."

As he started through the woods again, a gleaming object on the ground caught his eye. It was a heavy trap, half-concealed by a frond of ferns, its steel jaws set for prey. Joe's foot had just missed it!

He bent down to examine the trap. Judging from the condition of the rabbit-meat bait, it must have been set recently.

Suddenly Joe had the eerie feeling that he was being spied upon. He glanced ahead just in time to see the head of a man duck out of sight in a nearby thicket. The stranger had light-colored hair and sharp eyes. Though Joe had caught only a quick glimpse of the face, he knew that he had seen it before.

"The salesman at the Mortons' farm!" he muttered.

Joe raced after the retreating man. Realizing that it might be foolhardy to assume the chase alone, Joe gave a bird whistle that the Hardys often used as a signal.

Frank and Chet, farther upstream, heard the whistle and answered with a similar signal.

But so intent were they in trying to locate Joe's direction that they did not notice a ledge of submerged rock until it was too late. The jagged ledge tore a gaping hole in the canvas a few feet behind the prow of the canoe. Water came pouring in.

His foot just missed the trap!

Frank strained at the crude paddle to drive the canoe ashore. Despite their efforts, water was halfway to the gunwales when the bow scraped the pebbly bottom of the left bank.

"Whew! Just made it!" Chet exclaimed.

"Wait here!" Frank said, then dashed downstream along the bank. The whistle sounded again!

Within a few seconds Frank found himself at a sharp bend in the river. Joe was nowhere in sight. Frank whistled. There was no reply.

"Where'd he go?" Frank murmured.

He hoped his brother was not in danger. But where to look for him was a puzzle.

Frank decided to go back to Chet. Joe might have headed in that direction.

"Didn't you find Joe?" Chet asked, wide-eyed.

"Not yet. The sound seemed to come from both sides of the stream," Frank replied, perplexed. "I hope it doesn't mean somebody was imitating our bird call."

Chet mopped his brow. "Gosh, if that happened, then the fellow who left the warning must be on our trail!" he exclaimed, glancing anxiously at the woods about him.

Suddenly his eyes were attracted by something rising above the treetops.

"Frank! Pigeons!"

Two white birds rose high, circled for several seconds, then headed south. A startling thought struck Frank. Were these pigeons from the same covey as the ones sent to the Hardy home? If so, then the kidnappers might have their hideout near this very spot!

Maybe Joe had stumbled upon the men by accident and run into trouble!

As the two birds disappeared from view, another pair of pigeons came into sight. Like the others, they started to circle when suddenly a blast cut the forest stillness and echoed and reechoed through the trees.

"A shot!" Frank exclaimed.

Chet cried out, "One of the pigeons must have been winged!"

The bird wheeled, then plummeted through the trees, while the other soared away.

"I'm going to find out who's here," Frank declared.

"Then I'll go with you," Chet offered, and trailed behind Frank.

"That shot sounded no more than a couple of hundred feet away," Frank whispered. "Easy now."

As they stepped carefully from tree trunk to tree trunk to avoid presenting themselves as targets, Frank's attention was attracted to a red cylinder on the ground. He picked it up.

"Look, Chet! A shotgun shell!"

Chet surveyed the woodland with quickening pulse. Perhaps the barrel of a gun was being aimed at them at that very second! He searched the area carefully, but could see no one.

A score of paces farther on, Frank found the pigeon, lying dead on a big boulder.

"It really caught a load of lead," he observed, lifting the limp, still-warm body of the bird.

There were no bands of identification on the pigeon, nor a message tube. This fact strengthened Frank's suspicion that these birds, too, belonged to the criminals who had telephoned the ransom message.

He was relieved by the fact that there had been only one shot. At least Joe had not been under fire.

But presently Frank's imagination got the better of him. He visualized Joe being hustled off through the woods, his hands high in the air, and a shotgun prodding him in the back. Frank's reverie was brought to a sudden end by the spine-chilling howl of a dog, and the wild yell of a human being calling for help. Both sounds ended as suddenly as they had started.

"Th-that was Joe!" quavered Chet.

Frank did not reply. With a furious burst of speed he dashed among the trees toward the direction from which the sound had come, unmindful of the brambles that tore at his clothes or the low-hanging branches that stung his cheeks. Chet panted after him as fast as his weight and the pack would allow.

Abruptly Frank found himself on a fairly well-beaten trail. He sped along it.

"Wait! Wait for me!" Chet cried.

The Hardy boy slackened his speed. Chet caught up to him at a spot where the trail cut through a dense growth of bushes.

"Come on!" he urged.

The two boys dashed among the bushes. A second later the ground seemed to drop away from beneath their feet.

Frank and Chet plunged helplessly downward!

CHAPTER X

The Detector

SLOWLY Frank opened his eyes. He was lying in a tangled mass of brush and sod.

"Where am I?" he said half-aloud.

The boy moved his right hand and felt someone lying beside him. Then he sensed a crushing pressure on his legs.

Frank rubbed his hand over his forehead to clear his brain. Memory came back with a rush. He had been running with Chet. Then that awful drop. Now he found himself lying at the bottom of a deep pit.

Summoning every ounce of strength in his body, Frank raised himself up on one elbow. In the gloom of the pit he peered at the body beside him.

"Joe!" he cried in surprise.

His brother lay there, unconscious.

In trying to rise, Frank realized that the weight

on his legs was Chet. Frank rumpled the boy's hair.

"Chet! Chet! Are you all right?"

In a few seconds Chet's eyes opened. "Where are we? How did we get here?" he asked in bewilderment.

"We plunged into a pit of some kind. Here's Joe."

"Joe? How'd he—?" Then Chet realized that Joe was unconscious.

"We've got to get him out of here," said Frank.

The pit into which they had fallen was deep and narrow. Frank and Chet had trouble worming their way to a standing position. As Frank bent down to place his hands beneath his brother's shoulders, Joe stirred. He shook his head dazedly and tried to sit up.

"Attaboy," Frank said. "Take it easy."

"Oh, that wolf!" Joe groaned.

"What wolf?" Chet asked.

"The one that chased me." Joe looked around. In a few seconds his mind cleared completely. "Oh, yes, I fell in here. It's a good thing you found me."

"We didn't find you," Chet said with a rueful grin. "We fell in, too!"

"Well, let's get out of here," Joe pleaded, although he felt pretty unsteady.

"Golly, it's eight feet deep if it's an inch," Chet moaned.

Climb on my shoulders, Chet," Frank suggested. "Once you're topside, you can haul us up."

"Look out for snipers," Joe warned.

Chet climbed to Frank's shoulders and stood on this teetering perch, with Frank grasping the boy's ankles to steady him. Chet peered around. Seeing no one, he wriggled over the top.

"Ready?" he called down.

"Okay."

As Frank braced himself again, Joe sprang up. In a moment he, too, was out of the pit. With Joe helping Chet keep his balance, the stout boy pulled Frank from the hole.

The three of them sprawled on the ground to get their breath back and to take stock of their injuries. They were relieved to find that aside from a few minor scratches and bruises all were unhurt.

"What were you doing way off here?" Frank asked his brother.

Joe told about the steel trap in which he had nearly caught his foot, then of spotting the man who had probably set it.

"I'm certain that he's the same guy who followed you from the newspaper office and who posed as a salesman that morning at Chet's farm."

"Ow-ee, I don't like this," Chet said. "Where'd he go?"

"When he saw me, he started to run. He sure led me a chase across the river and back."

"What was it you said about a wolf?" Chet asked. "We heard one howl."

"And what a howl!" Joe said. "I yelled for help!"

He added that just before he had pitched into the hole, the ferocious beast had come crashing through the woods and raced after him.

"One of the wild dogs of North Woods!" Chet exclaimed.

"It was a close race," Joe said. "Maybe it was a good thing I fell into this hole!"

"Holy crow!" Frank exclaimed as a thought suddenly occurred to him. "Do you realize this hole was covered with brush when we fell in?"

"N-never thought of that," Chet said. "Then somebody sneaked up after Joe was trapped and covered it up again!"

"Right. Maybe the idea was to catch all three of us and then . . ."

"He may be coming back to capture us right now," Chet said, struggling to his feet. "Let's leave, pronto."

The boys needed food and rest before they would be able to continue their search for the missing rifles and to find out what mischief the pseudosalesman was up to and why everybody was so determined to scare them out of the North Woods.

As they made their way back to the canoe, Chet told Joe how it had rammed a rock. Suddenly a grim thought struck him. "I'll bet the canoe and pack are gone!" he said.

Fearing that Chet's dire prediction might be true, the Hardys quickened their pace.

"It's a long hike back to the other fellows," Chet moaned. "It would be dark before we could get to camp, and these gangsters—"

Just then the boys reached the bank of the stream and Joe called out: "Chet, you were wrong. The canoe is still here!"

"Whew!" breathed Chet, vastly relieved.

The boys quickly patched the canoe. "Not bad!" Joe said approvingly.

"If we don't hit any more rocks, I guess we can make camp."

They shoved off, taking the same positions as they had on the trip up. It was easier traveling with the current. Keeping a sharp lookout for underwater rocks, the Hardys deftly steered the canoe while Chet sat relaxed in the bottom, his hands behind his head.

"How large was the wolf that chased you, Joe?" he asked.

"About four feet long."

Joe said he had a hunch that the wolf might belong to the blond man, who probably called him off after seeing Joe fall.

Frank recounted his and Chet's experiences, ending with the pigeon episode.

"At least one thing seems certain," he said in

conclusion. "The thieves who stole Chet's truck were also my kidnappers—or at least they're in cahoots with them."

"It wouldn't surprise me," Joe said, "if their hideout isn't far from here."

Chet winced. Then suddenly he beamed. "Hey, fellows, I see camp!" he announced. A tantalizing aroma filled the air. "Food!" he exclaimed as the canoe grounded on the shore close by the camp.

Biff and Tony, seeing their friends' bruises and disheveled clothes, fired questions in rapid succession, growing more amazed as each was answered.

"Those men sure must want to keep people away from North Woods," Tony remarked.

"You might have been killed," Biff said.

As they ate, the boys conjectured about what underhanded schemes the pit digger might be carrying on, but could figure out nothing except that for one reason or another he wanted to prevent people from entering a certain section of the woods.

"Tomorrow we'll track him down and find out!" Frank said with determination.

Suddenly the boys realized that Chet had been missing since they had finished eating. After a brief search they saw him on the far side of the pond, a fishing rod in his hands. After he had cast, Frank came up behind him.

"Where'd you get the swell rod?" Frank asked.

"Found it. Pretty nifty, eh? Practically new."

Chet jumped as he realized that under the circumstances this rod meant more than its loss by a careless fisherman. It might be the property of the fellow who had left the warning the night before.

"Any identification on that fishing rod?" Frank asked.

Chet looked. "Say, Frank, this came from Wells Hardware Store! Here's the name."

"I'm sure the owner didn't mean to leave it," Frank observed as the boys walked back. "You know, Chet, this might be a means of finding out what the thief looks like."

"How?"

"I'll bet he was buying this rod when you were in the store. He may have heard you talking to the clerk. Right?"

Chet admitted he had bragged about his big-game-hunter uncle and the rifles. There had been several customers in the store at the time, but he had paid no attention to them.

"Gee, if only I had!" he said ruefully as they returned to camp.

Frank thought there was a good chance the mysterious fisherman would return for the rod during the night, and suggested they stay on watch.

"Anyway, we won't be in danger of a surprise attack," Frank said. "After this, we'll use the sound detector we brought. Good thing you thought of it, Joe."

"I didn't know you had one," Biff said.

"The gadget belongs to Dad, but he let us borrow it," Joe said.

Frank opened his pack and drew out the detector. It was the size of a cigarette case, but one could plainly hear sounds far beyond the range of the human ear. During the late afternoon and evening the boys took turns listening.

"You could almost hear the guys breathe with this gimmick," Tony said. "It's great!"

No sounds of particular interest were picked up, and at nine o'clock Frank put the detector in his pack.

"Think I'll hit the sack," he told the others.

"Me too," said Joe. "Biff, arrange the watches, will you?"

After two-hour shifts had been agreed upon, Biff turned on his radio for news of the missing Jack Wayne. The announcer said there was still no clue to the whereabouts of the pilot, although the search was still being carried on over the ocean.

"That means they've given up looking around here," said Joe, wriggling into his bag.

The boys fell asleep, with Biff on guard. Frank took his turn in the early morning. So far there had been no prowlers. Soon a rosy tint covered the eastern sky.

"We should get started on our sleuthing soon," he told himself an hour later as he prepared three small emergency kits with knives, rope, first-aid articles, and some food.

He roused the others, and it was not long before he, Joe, and Biff had finished breakfast and were ready to shove off in the canoe. Chet and Tony would remain at camp in case anyone should show up for the fishing rod.

When the three boys started off, a light mist hung over the river and drifted among the trees. By the time the sun had burned the mist away, they had reached the spot where Chet and Frank had seen the pigeons the day before.

The boys carried the canoe a hundred feet inland and concealed it in a thicket.

"Let's start from the pit and work north," Joe suggested. "That blond fellow I followed was headed in that direction."

They started forward cautiously. Frank turned on the sound detector and listened intently. He reported bird calls and insect sounds, but no human voices. In a short time the hikers came to the trail which led to the pit. As they neared it, Joe called excitedly:

"The hole's covered over again!"

Frank put the detector to his ear. No sounds came from it except those of the woodland creatures and the distant murmur of the stream.

Spreading out twenty feet apart, the boys moved along silently. Frank stopped every few seconds to listen.

Then suddenly the youth raised his hand for the others to stop. Biff and Joe came over to him. "I hear something different, but it's very faint," he said in a low voice.

Careful not to make any noise, the boys proceeded in the direction of the mysterious sound. A hundred feet farther he halted again.

"You take this gadget, Joe, and tell me what you think it is."

Joe listened. "Sounds like pounding or hammering," he said.

"I thought it might be a machine," Frank said. "You listen, Biff."

After holding the detector to his ear a few seconds the lanky youth grinned. "I don't hear anything like that. You fellows spoofing me?"

Joe grabbed the instrument and listened for a minute. "The sound has stopped."

Frank frowned. "Maybe we've been seen. From now on we'd better creep along," he advised.

"Yeah, we may be right on top of their hideout," Biff said grimly.

The ground ahead rose slightly to the crown of a little hillock. Reaching the top, the boys peered hopefully down the other side.

"Do you see what I see?" Frank whispered excitedly. "Isn't that a chimney sticking up behind those trees? Come on, fellows!"

The boys made their way down the hill, taking extreme care to keep well concealed.

"Let's sneak up on the place from three directions," Biff said.

The chimney belonged to an old shack. The roof was half caved in, and gunny sacks were nailed over the windows.

"Guess nobody lives here," Biff observed.

"Somebody may be hiding in it, though," said Frank. "We'd better find out."

The boys conferred briefly on making a surprise attack. It was decided that Joe would throw a rock at the back of the cabin. If anybody were inside, his attention would be directed there. Then Frank and Biff would rush in through the front door.

Well hidden in the bushes, Joe selected a large rock. Taking careful aim, he sent it sailing toward the building. It hit with a loud crash. Immediately Frank and Biff raced from cover and ran through the front entrance.

Nobody was inside. The only sign of habitation was a rickety cot, which showed no evidence of recent use. On a crude hearth lay a heap of ashes. Frank felt the stones. They were cold. By this time Joe had joined them.

"Nobody home," Biff announced.

"What's that?" Joe asked as he noticed a large object, draped with burlap bags, standing in a corner. He pulled them off, revealing a motor.

"Holy crow!" he exclaimed. "It's an airplane engine. How did it get here?"

An idea flashed into Biff's mind. "The missing plane! Maybe it crashed in these woods after all, and somebody dragged the motor in here!"

"It couldn't have been dragged far," Joe said excitedly. "This thing is heavy. I'll bet Jack Wayne's nearby. Come on, fellows. Let's look for him!"

CHAPTER XI

A Hoax

"If Jack Wayne crashed here," Frank said, "the person who moved the motor would have taken care of him, too."

"The gang!" Joe declared. "Maybe that's what Wayne meant by 'hijackers.' "

Biff had a different idea. "Wayne may not be here at all. That motor could have torn loose from the plane before it crashed."

"Hey!" Frank called out excitedly. "This motor has never been in a plane. It's brand new! I should have noticed that right away!"

"How do you suppose they ever got an airplane engine through these woods?" asked Joe.

The three boys scouted the area for further evidence, agreeing to meet again at the cabin to report any sign of a plane accident or other unusual circumstance. Joe, the first to return, had seen nothing unusual, except that a piece of bark had been chipped off a tree standing near the shack.

Wondering if the cut had any special significance, he looked at other trees in the vicinity. Three of them had had bits of bark stripped off.

Joe was about to look farther, when Frank and Biff joined him. After hearing they had failed to locate a crack-up, he called their attention to the nicked trees.

"I believe they're trail-blaze marks," he said, "and made not very long ago. Let's follow 'em and see where they lead."

Within five minutes two other marked trees were found.

"Do you think the trail might lead to the wrecked plane?" Biff asked.

The Hardys were inclined to believe the trail might possibly take them near the hideout of the men they were seeking. The boys continued to follow it.

The Hardys' keen eyes were alert for any evidence that the thieves or kidnappers might be around. But by midmorning all were weary from following the blazed trees with no end to the trail. Frank kept listening to the detector, but if the forest held a secret, it was being kept well.

All at once Biff let out a cry. "Well, what do you know about this? We've been going in a circle."

Frank and Joe rushed to where their friend stood. There was no doubt about it. An oak with some of its bark removed was easily identified by a long split down the trunk into which a bird had built a nest.

Following a trampled path, the boys found another familiar tree, then another.

"I don't see why anybody would mark a trail in a circle," Biff said.

After a few minutes' thought Frank suggested that there probably were offshoots of the main trail. The boys spread out to look. Only Biff found one.

"This thing's got me dizzy," he said. "Where are we headed, anyway?"

Frank stopped. "I think there's something phony about this whole deal," he said. "Maybe this trail was made on purpose to lead people away from the cabin or the place where we heard the hammering sound."

"You mean I'm going to fall into some trap the way you fellows did?" Biff exclaimed, frowning.

"Not if you watch your step," Joe replied.

The boys walked on. More trail marks, and more unfamiliar territory. Silence followed, until Frank whispered:

"I've picked up something on the detector. Sounds like digging. Somebody's up ahead, and not far away!"

The hikers dropped to the ground, then slowly and silently inched their way forward.

Biff, in his enthusiasm to make a capture, outdistanced the others.

Ahead loomed a large rock. The unknown digger was on the other side of it. The boys could hear the sound of metal biting into soil.

"Here goes!" Biff murmured to himself.

He raised up and flung himself upon the stooped figure. There was a tangle of arms and legs. The digger was overpowered. Biff peered into his face.

"Chet! Well, I'll be mousetrapped," he blurted, rising from the stout boy's midriff.

"What are you doing here?" Frank asked.

"Yes, how did you get this far from camp?" Joe put in eagerly.

"W-w-wait a minute," Chet begged. "Let me catch my breath."

He sat down against the rock and mopped his brow. "I do a fellow a favor," he continued, "and this is what happens."

"Do whom a favor?" Frank asked.

"Tony. Who else?" Chet puffed. "I'm digging worms for him. He wants to catch some trout."

The boys looked down at the hole. Chet had been digging with his tin plate. Two worms wriggled beside it.

"Where's Tony?" Frank asked.

"At camp. Right over there!"

"Oh no!" Joe wailed.

"Jumpin' jeepers!" Biff exclaimed. "Somebody made a trail right here to our camp!"

"He probably was watching all the time," Joe

declared. "But if he was one of the gang, why didn't he just shoot at us and get it over with?"

"I don't think the trail was made by one of the gang," Frank said. "We may have a friend in North Woods."

"What do you mean?" Chet asked.

"That warning note we received may have been left by someone with good intentions, and he's helped us out again."

After hearing the whole story, Chet said, "Two warnings are enough for me. I vote we leave this place."

"I think Chet's right," Biff said. "Let's shove off."

Tony agreed with Chet and Biff. "What's more," he said, "my dad's expecting me home to drive for him."

Outvoted, the Hardys agreed to go, but begged the others to stay until morning.

"Look, fellows," Frank said, "Joe and I will do some work alone. You fellows stay here and swim. Besides, we have to get the canoe."

They ate a quick lunch from the emergency kit they were carrying, then made their way to the tumble-down shack. They approached it quietly, Frank in the lead.

"Joe! The motor's gone!"

The boys stared in amazement at the spot where the engine had stood. The burlap sacks had been tossed to one side.

"Gosh, I wish I'd taken the serial number of that engine," Joe said.

"I wonder how much of a gang is in on this deal," Frank mused. "It would take several strong men to move that heavy engine. Well, now where do we head?"

The boys decided to depend on the detector for help. Finally their patience bore fruit.

"Hammering?" Joe asked as his brother's face lighted up.

"No."

"The wailing siren?"

Frank shook his head. "An animal."

Joe listened. "Maybe it's the wolf that attacked me," he said.

"If he belongs to that fake salesman, now's our chance to find that crook!" Frank declared.

Hunting knives in hand to assist in any unexpected attack, the boys started off in the direction of the howling, which now could be heard without the aid of the detector.

"That's more than one animal," Frank said.

The Hardys proceeded more slowly. Suddenly a clearing opened up ahead. In the middle of it the boys saw a six-foot-high wire enclosure. Behind the netting five animals growled fiercely.

"Wolves!" Joe exclaimed.

"Sure looks that way," Frank answered.

"What are they doing here?"

"We'll find out."

Careful to keep themselves concealed, the boys circled the enclosure. The wolves smelled their presence, however, and started to howl.

"I hope they haven't given us away," Joe whispered. "Their keeper must be nearby."

The boys looked about them. Partly hidden among the trees some distance to their left was a cabin, its front door open.

Frank and Joe approached it cautiously. Nobody was in sight.

"Someone may be spying on us from a window," Joe whispered.

He and Frank waited a few minutes before approaching closer to the cabin. Nothing seemed to be stirring.

"I'm going to take a look," Joe said.

"I'm with you."

They stepped quietly through the brush and into a small open space in front of the cabin. There was an ominous silence about the place.

Anxiety showed on Frank's face. "Joe, I don't like . . ."

His words were punctured by a snarl which froze the boys in their tracks. The head of a wolf flashed in the doorway. With a vicious growl, it sprang toward the Hardys.

"The same one that attacked me!" thought Joe, poising his knife.

The beast let out a piercing whine and jerked back. Then the boys saw that he was chained to

the door. The frustrated animal continued to bel-
low and glower, straining at his leash.

A sharp voice cut the air. *"Stand where you
are!"*

Frank and Joe wheeled. A tall man, his hat
pulled low, stood before them, a gun in his hand.

CHAPTER XII

A Strange Pet

THE man was a giant of a woodsman. His face was heavily bearded and his eyes fiercely sharp. Besides the gun, he carried a long whip.

"What are you doing here?" he demanded.

"Oh—uh—just looking around," Frank replied, trying to look innocent. "I'm afraid we're lost."

The man eyed the boys sharply, as if he doubted this statement.

"You're trespassing on private property," he said sternly.

"Private?" Joe asked.

"Yes. I breed wolves here. This is a dangerous area."

All the while the animal chained to the door growled and pulled at his leash.

"Quiet, Saber!" the man shouted.

He flicked his whip and the end of it snapped

like a rifle shot a scant two inches from the wolf's jaws. The animal retreated and threw itself down across the doorway.

"Why do you keep wolves here?" Joe asked.

"I breed them for zoos. And now I want to give you kids some good advice," he snapped. "Leave this forest pronto and don't come back! Do you hear me? *Don't come back!*"

Frank was not ready to go quite yet. This man might know some things the Hardys wanted to find out.

"Do you take care of these animals all alone?" he asked.

"Yes."

"Oh, by the way, we found a valuable rod and reel near our camp down near the river. Do you know who may have left it there?"

"No."

"Did a plane crash around here recently?" Joe queried.

"No."

"There's an old shack off in the woods," Frank said, pointing to the direction from which they had come. "Anybody live there?"

"Listen, I ain't answering any more of your nebby questions," the woodsman said curtly. "Now clear out of here and don't let me see you around these parts again!" He cracked his whip. "Get going!"

Joe thrust out his chin in determination. "We'll go," he said, "but we don't intend to be ordered around like your animals!"

The man merely glared as the Hardys retreated into the woods, following the trail over which they had come. When they were out of earshot of the woodsman, they stopped to talk over the situation.

"I sure don't care for that guy!" Joe said.

"Same here. I wouldn't trust him as far as I could throw a haystack," Frank agreed.

"His story about breeding wolves for zoos sounded awfully fishy."

"Of course. It's obvious he's training the wolves to attack people. But why?"

"Probably to scare them out of the woods. The critter that chased me just before I fell into the pit looked an awful lot like Saber," Joe said.

Suddenly Frank stiffened. "Listen!"

In the distance he had detected the sound of something crashing through the brush.

"Saber!" Joe exclaimed. "The man let him loose!"

"Up a tree!" Frank urged.

The boys raced through the forest until they spotted a couple of fir trees they could climb readily. Leaping to the lowest branches, they pulled themselves up into the trees.

The Hardys were barely a safe distance off the ground when Saber reached them. Snarling and snapping, he pawed at one trunk and then the other. Joe broke off a branch and hurled it down, hitting the wolf on the nose. The infuriated animal howled and ran in circles around the tree.

"This beast may not let us down for days," Joe remarked woefully.

"There's one way we can catch him," Frank said hopefully. "With a pole and noose. There's a branch above you that's pretty straight."

Joe climbed up. He cut off the branch and quickly stripped it of twigs and leaves.

"I have a coil of small rope in my pocket," Frank said, pulling it out.

He threw it across to Joe, who fastened a noose to the end of the pole.

Joe dangled the pole and the noose close to the ground. The wolf snapped at it. With a deft twist, the boy flung the rope over Saber's head.

"Pull!" Frank cried.

The boy hauled the pole upward, but the wolf was heavy. It lashed out fiercely, snarling and gnashing with its fangs. Suddenly the animal freed itself and tumbled to the ground.

"Whew!" Joe exclaimed. "He weighs a ton."

Saber continued to circle the trees but more warily. Joe tried to rope him again, but the wolf would not be tricked the second time.

As the boys wondered what to do, they were startled by a distant wailing noise.

"What's that, Frank? The siren?"

"Sounds like it, but it's mighty faint."

"Well, what do you know about that?" Joe cried. "Saber's leaving!"

The strange sound seemed to bother the animal. Putting its tail between its legs, Saber slunk off.

"He acts frightened. That sound probably hurts his ears."

The boys dropped to the ground. "Gosh, I thought I was going to have to live in that tree." Joe grinned as he stretched his legs. "Let's get back to camp."

The Hardys found their way to the spot where the canoe was cached. They slid it into the water and paddled rapidly downstream. By the time they rejoined the other boys, the sun was sinking behind the trees to the west.

Chet, Biff, and Tony rushed to the shore to meet their friends.

As Frank and Joe related their adventures, Chet's mouth sagged open.

"A wolf?" he asked in disbelief. "If he picks up our scent, he'll come right into this camp. What say, fellows? Let's get out of here!"

Frank and Joe were fairly sure that even if Saber had picked up their trail, he would get no farther than the place they had put the canoe into the water.

"But to make sure he doesn't bother us again, we'll have to catch the critter," Joe said determinedly. "With a stockade. We'll build one after chow. How about it, Tony? Do we have trout tonight?"

"Six nice fat rainbows," Tony told him. "Biff and I caught 'em."

"With my worms," Chet added.

The boys laughed and joked through the meal. When it was over, Frank said:

"Now to work on the stockade. We'll need saplings—plenty of 'em."

A number of small trees grew along the stream and the boys made short work of felling them. Soon a pile of saplings, stripped of their branches, lay on the spot which the Hardys had selected for the trap.

While the others were digging a small trench, Joe and Frank went into the woods for vines with which to tie the saplings together. It did not take the boys long to erect a crude stockade. Frank arranged a small opening on one side with a gate which would drop in place once an animal had entered the trap.

"Now all we need is bait," Joe said.

"I've some meat that we won't need," Tony said. "We can use that." He produced a sizable chunk left over from the piece which the boys had taken along for stew.

"That's perfect," Frank said.

He fastened the meat to a long string, which, when pulled, would cause the gate to fall shut.

They tried it several times to be sure the trap would work.

"Saber ought to tackle this meat before he does us," Joe said. "I hope this trap's strong enough to hold him. I don't want to be his dessert."

The site of the trap was some distance from the camp, but the boys could see it from where they sat around the fire exchanging observations on the day's events. When darkness began to fall, Joe got up and stretched sleepily.

"I'm going to tumble in, fellows," he said. "I'll take a morning watch."

"Me, too." Biff yawned.

As Joe rose from the ground, he cried hoarsely, "Fellows, the stockade!"

All heads swung to the direction of the trap where two glowing eyes moved slowly toward the gateway.

CHAPTER XIII

Another Theft

THE boys heard the stockade gate drop. This was followed by a howling so wild and terrifying that the forest itself seemed to shudder.

Biff and Tony started running toward the stockade.

"Easy," Frank warned. "Let the beast tire himself out before we take a look."

Excitedly the boys stood by while the trapped animal thrashed about. It jumped at the walls of the stockade, making the saplings quiver under each assault. Finally the wolf's rage subsided into snarling submission.

"All right, now," Frank said. "We'll see what we caught."

Beaming their flashlights ahead of them, the boys warily approached the stockade. When they reached the side of it, Joe dropped down on hands and knees.

"Stand on my back," he said to Frank, "and take a gander over the top."

Carefully Frank trained his flashlight and peered down from the top of the sapling wall. A large wolf, a heavy collar around its neck, crouched in one corner of the stockade. Its tongue hung out and foam flecked the cruel mouth.

"Saber!" Frank said. "Just as we thought."

The boys took turns looking down at the trembling animal.

"Th-that's the thing which chased you and Joe?" Chet said to Frank. "Boy, am I glad I stayed in camp!"

"What are we going to do with it?" Biff asked.

He received no immediate answer because Frank and Joe were conferring in low tones near the gate of the stockade.

"We don't have the upper hand here by a long shot," Frank was saying.

"I see what you mean," Joe replied. "Saber's master is probably nearby."

"Right. If only he wasn't armed! We're no match against a man with a gun, Joe!"

The boys decided to put on an act for the benefit of Saber's owner. In a loud voice Frank called out:

"Fellows, let's get out of here! This woods is no place for campers, even with Saber out of circulation."

"We'll go at the crack of dawn," Joe agreed

"Saber!" Frank said. "Just as we thought!"

loudly. "I don't like the idea of being chewed up." Then he whispered to his brother, "But we'll come back here without that woodsman knowing about it. Maybe we'll have better luck next time."

Guard duty was arranged, but the night passed uneventfully.

The next morning it was decided that Chet, Tony, and Biff would take the canoe and most of the camp equipment downstream. The river must eventually flow into the sea, probably near Barmet Bay.

"Joe and I'll hike back through the woods," Frank said. "We'll pick up the car, and contact you when we arrive home."

"What shall we do about Saber?" Joe asked. "We don't dare let him out, but we can't leave him to starve."

Frank said grimly, "I'll bet that as soon as we go, his owner will come for him."

The Hardys shoved the laden canoe from shore and watched until their companions had paddled out of sight. Then they slung their packs over their shoulders and started back for the farm where they had left Chet's jalopy.

They had been on their way only a few minutes when Joe said, "Let's go back and see if the woodsman has released Saber. Are you game?"

Caching their packs in a thicket, the boys cautiously retraced their steps until they came to a big rock on a rise of ground. Peering around it, they were able to look down at the stockade. All was quiet except for the growl of the wolf. But as the boys watched, the animal suddenly grew restless, its growl climbing the scale to a thin whine.

"He hears somebody," Frank said.

"Us, maybe?"

"No. I think that whine means his master is around."

Suddenly they heard the distant sound of someone coming through the brush and flattened themselves on the ground to escape detection. Whoever it was, was making no effort to conceal his presence, certain that the campers had departed. The tramping of feet became louder, and someone approached the stockade.

"The woodsman!" Joe whispered.

The bearded man stopped, listened, then went to the gate of the stockade. Bending down, he lifted it, and when Saber's head appeared, he snapped a wire leash onto the animal's collar.

"Fool!" the boys heard the woodsman snarl. "Letting yourself get trapped by a bunch of kids." Then he cuffed the animal, which cringed at his feet. The wolf acted like a beaten puppy.

The man retreated a few paces from the stockade and stood glaring at it. Then he ran up and hurled his body full force against the saplings. They began to give way under the charge.

He repeated the performance and at length the wall crashed in. Angrily the man continued to batter the stockade until it was level with the ground. Then he set off with Saber.

"Whew!" Joe said when the man was out of sight. "Some temper! Well, let's make tracks! We know now that the wolf won't starve."

It was late in the afternoon before the Hardys reached the road where they had first entered the woods. From there they went straight to the farmhouse and retrieved the jalopy. After thanking the farm woman for letting them park there, the boys hopped in and started for home.

When they pulled up in front of their house, they found Chet sitting on the front steps, a piece of cake in one hand, a banana in the other.

"Hi, fellows!" he called out. "Got a lift into town, so I thought I'd pick up the jalopy."

Chet said the trip downstream had been uneventful. It had joined the Willow River, which emptied into the bay. Tony had telephoned his home from a waterfront restaurant, and Mrs. Prito had come to pick up the campers in her husband's small truck, and had delivered Chet and his canoe to the Morton home.

As soon as Chet had finished his cake, he decided to drive home. The two tired boys picked up their packs, mounted the front porch steps, and entered the house. Mrs. Hardy flung her arms around them.

"I'm glad you're back," she said. "Chet has been telling us the wildest tales about wolves and prison pits and—"

She was interrupted by Aunt Gertrude, who came bustling into the hall from the kitchen. "I'm glad you're back safe, too. But that Morton boy! I'd like to tie his tongue up, scaring your mother with such preposterous stories. I sent him outside with some food to stop his talking. Wolves in North Woods! Ridiculous! Why, there isn't a wolf outside of Siberia, except in a few zoos."

Frank and Joe looked at each other. Perhaps they had better not tell the whole story of what had happened, except to their father. Learning that he was working on a report in his study, the boys dashed upstairs.

"Hello, sons," Mr. Hardy said, smiling, and closed the door. "Now let's have the truth about your trip."

When the boys had finished the account of their adventures, their father asked a few questions. The point which seemed to interest him most concerned the pigeons.

"You're sure there was no message concealed on the one that was shot?" he asked. "Did you look under the tail feathers?"

The boys had to admit they had not thought to look anywhere but on the legs. Probably they had missed a good clue.

Mr. Hardy asked the boys to go outside and

look at the kidnappers' pigeon, which was in its cage in the garage.

"See if it's the same kind you saw in the woods."

Aunt Gertrude had appointed herself keeper and feeder of the bird. She went out with her nephews to show them what her good care and a well-selected diet had done for "the poor, emaciated bird" that had been delivered to them.

Suddenly Aunt Gertrude, in the lead, gave a shriek, then cried out:

"It's gone! The pigeon's gone!"

CHAPTER XIV

The Mysterious Light

THE pigeon's cage as well as the bird had disappeared. A pane of glass which had been removed from a rear window was mute evidence of how the thief had entered.

There was no question in the boys' minds as to who had taken the bird. It had to be one of Frank's kidnappers.

"But when? When?" Aunt Gertrude cried out. "I took the pigeon his supper not an hour ago."

She was extremely annoyed over the incident, and Mr. Hardy was vexed that they had missed another opportunity to learn who the pigeon's owner was.

"I should have followed that second pigeon to its cote. It might have helped considerably if we could have found its home."

The detective added that the happenings in

North Woods seemed to point to the fact that there was a connection between his own case and the guns and equipment stolen from the Morton truck.

"More marked bills have turned up in the United States," he said. "The FBI is sure the money is being used for some illegal purpose. But they don't know yet what it could be."

"But I'll bet you have a theory, Dad," Joe spoke up.

"Rifles."

"How did you figure that?"

The detective said his assumption was based on deduction rather than absolute proof. While in Washington he had heard that a dory containing United States rifles had been found on the coast of Central America.

"The dory had been wrecked in a storm," the detective said, "and the men who had manned it either drowned or swam off and left it. There was no mark of identification on the boat, but I believe it came from a large vessel."

"Smugglers," Frank commented. "Dad, do you think Tyler Morton's stolen rifles are on their way to the Caribbean?"

"You've given up the idea they're in North Woods?" His father smiled.

"No, I haven't. And Joe and I want to go back there. Will you go with us?"

"Yes. But first I think we'd better take a look at the area from the air."

"You mean scout the enemy before we attack?" Joe grinned. "Let's go right away."

"The sun is too low," his father said. "There'll be deep shadows over the woods at this time of day. We'll go tomorrow morning."

Frank made the arrangements, and at ten o'clock the next day the three Hardys were at the airport. A young man named Eric Martin, whom the boys knew, was assigned to pilot them.

"Hello," Joe said to him. "Any news from Wayne?"

Eric shook his head gravely. "Not a word since that hijacker message."

Mr. Hardy gave the young man instructions, and they took off. Leaving Bayport behind, the plane followed the Willow River, then took the tributary that headed into North Woods.

As the forest came into view, Frank pulled binoculars from his jacket. "I see the little pond where we went swimming," he reported presently.

"That means we're close to the wolf-man's hideout," Joe said.

"Yes, there's the pen in that clearing right below us," Frank replied. "Can't tell from this height if any wolves are in it or not."

"And there's the shack where we saw the airplane engine," Joe remarked.

The plane crisscrossed the area, but nothing suspicious came into view.

"Take her down to a thousand feet," Mr. Hardy told the pilot.

The plane banked and descended.

Frank handed the binoculars to his father, but the detective could see nothing save the dense, uneven forest below.

"Those gangsters must have some kind of camp," Joe said.

"If any of them are in the North Woods," said his father, "they're taking every precaution not to have their camp spotted from the air. But I was hoping we might find something else."

"Like what?"

"Smoke, a camouflaged building, trees or vegetation arranged in some significant pattern. I suppose we may as well turn back."

After the plane had landed and the Hardys were driving home, they made plans to leave together directly after lunch for a more careful search through North Woods. As they walked into the house, Mrs. Hardy handed her husband a telegram. He tore it open, read it swiftly, and frowned.

"I've been called back to Washington," he said. "I'll have to catch a plane. This is urgent."

Mr. Hardy said he would be gone only one day. He suggested that his sons keep busy on the case.

"Sure, Dad. How?" Frank asked.

"Suppose you circle the entire woodland area in your car. It's close to seventy miles all the way around, I'd say, and there may be another trail that's a shortcut to the thieves' camp.

"Talk to people who live on the edge of the woods," his father continued. "Perhaps they can provide you with some clues."

The young detectives started out in their car after lunch. When they reached the outskirts of North Woods, the good roads came to an end, and they began bouncing over rutted, narrow dirt roads.

"Pretty rugged out here," Frank said.

They stopped at every house whose acreage bordered the woodland. Most of the farmers had no interest in the forest and knew little about it, except that a fox would sneak out now and then to kill their chickens.

About four o'clock the boys drew up beside a stooped man walking along the road. He was very friendly but tired looking, as if he had been guiding a plow all day.

"Hello," Joe greeted him. "Can we give you a ride?"

The farmer whipped out a red bandanna to wipe his forehead. "Art's the name. And thanks, but I turn down this lane."

Frank spoke of their interest in the woods. The man eyed the boys with a skeptical half-smile.

"Them woods is a good place to stay clear of, I

always tell folks. Why, out yonder there's a pit full of snakes; hundreds of 'em wriggling around like they was crazy!"

Frank and Joe looked at each other as the man continued, "Then there's those wild dogs, too. Ain't never seen 'em, but on clear nights I hear 'em."

"Anybody live in North Woods?" Frank asked.

"Not that I ever heerd tell of, son."

The boys thanked the farmer and drove on to the next place. They found its owner as full of wild tales as his neighbor. He had been told that any humans or farm animals straying into the forest were never seen alive again, though their cries of agony could be heard for miles.

"Did you ever hear any?" Frank asked.

"No. But once I did hear a siren—like a fire-engine siren—and right after that there was a glow over the trees, just like the Northern Lights."

This man was sure no one lived in the forest any longer. The whole tract had been bought up by a lumber company years before, he told them. There were rumors that strangers had been seen on one of the old woods roads—surveyors, most likely. The boys drove off, excited by what they had heard.

"What do you think of that siren-and-light story, Frank?"

"If we hadn't heard the siren ourselves, and seen the wolves, I'd say all the stories were yarns.

I'm sure the other rumors were circulated by people who want to keep visitors out of North Woods."

Joe was all for going into the forest at once and having another look at the wolf-man's place.

Frank shook his head, "Nobody'd know where we were. And, anyway, an order from Dad is—"

"You're right. Let's finish our job."

The boys made a complete circuit of the forest, but found no trails that looked as though they had recently been used. The only new clue the day had yielded was the matter of the unexplained lights. Both boys were puzzled.

"Joe, it's the second time there's been a connection between a sudden flash of lights and a wailing siren," Frank said. "Do you suppose the one that night on the ocean, when every light on the yacht suddenly blazed up, could have anything to do with North Woods?"

Joe grinned. "You're stretching my imagination, but you probably mean that the plane could have signaled and the lights were an answer both times?"

"Exactly. When the siren wailed over North Woods, the trees were too thick for us to see any lights."

"But we didn't hear a helicopter."

"That's correct! So we're right back where we started from, which is exactly nowhere."

Frank switched on the car radio, hoping for

good news of Jack Wayne. But again the report was disappointing, and the announcer said hope for the flier was waning. The Hardys were silent the rest of the way home.

Frank pulled into the driveway and drove the car into the garage. He and Joe jumped out and made for the back steps, but the door swung open before they had reached it. Mrs. Hardy came out, obviously agitated.

"Frank! Joe!" she cried out. "I'm so glad you're back."

"What's the matter, Mother?"

"It's Chet. He's been telephoning every few minutes for the past half-hour."

"Why?"

"He's in trouble. Needs your help right away!"

CHAPTER XV

An Urgent Plea

CHET in trouble again!

"Did he say what about?" Joe asked.

Mrs. Hardy shook her head. "But he wants you to go right over to the farm."

"I wonder if it has anything to do with the stolen rifles," Frank mused.

"We'll soon find out," Joe replied as he ran back toward the garage with Frank behind him.

"Just a minute," their mother called. "One of you has to go to the hotel. Sam Radley's waiting for these letters." She handed Frank several envelopes for Mr. Hardy's operative, adding that the detective had something that he wanted brought back.

"Okay," Frank said. "Joe, you go to Chet's. I'll be back here in twenty minutes. If you need any help at the Mortons', call me."

When Frank returned from the errand, he found his mother even more disturbed than before.

"Chet phoned again," she said. "He told me what the trouble is. Actually, it's a family matter. Chet says they must have two thousand five hundred dollars tonight. Mr. Morton is away on business for the Dairymen's League and Chet says his mother begs us to lend her at least two thousand dollars of it until he comes home. The banks are open this evening. Chet will drive over for the money in three-quarters of an hour. Poor boy, he was so confused he could hardly talk."

"Did you talk to Mrs. Morton, Mother?" Frank asked.

"No, dear," she replied. "Chet said she couldn't come to the telephone."

"Mother, you didn't fall for a line like that!" Frank exclaimed. "Chet's mother would never ask for a loan of that much money!"

Mrs. Hardy looked at her tall son in amazement as he continued.

"The person who will call for the money will be the one who lost the two thousand dollars we found. This is our chance to catch him!"

Mrs. Hardy was unconvinced. Despite the fact that she had the utmost confidence in Frank's judgment, she was the type of woman, who, when a friend was in need, would make any sacrifice to help. Besides, she was sure the voice on the telephone had been Chet's. And he would not deliberately deceive her.

"It's something to do with a relative. Chet didn't seem to want to explain, and I got the feeling that the Mortons didn't care to tell us why they needed the money."

"All right," her son said, putting an arm around his mother's shoulder. "I know you're generous and sympathetic, but we can easily check on Chet's story. I'm going to telephone Joe. He should be at the Mortons' by this time."

He quickly dialed Chet's number. It was several seconds before the boy picked up the receiver.

"Hello? . . . Frank?"

"Is Joe there? Put him on."

"Y-yes."

"Say, Joe, what's the story about the two thousand five hundred dollars? It's not a phony?"

"It isn't phony," Joe replied. "I believe we ought to lend the Mortons the money."

"What! Where's Mrs. Morton?"

"Out. She's getting the other five hundred dollars."

"You really think we should do this?" Frank asked.

"Yes."

"All right. Tell Chet I'll bring it out."

"No, don't do that," Joe replied. "Chet will pick it up."

"You're coming, too?"

"Sure."

Frank hung up. He was perplexed. Maybe the request was legitimate, after all.

As a result of the conversation, Mrs. Hardy hastened to her desk in the corner of the living room. She drew out her savings account passbook and filled out a withdrawal form.

Her son put the book and withdrawal slip in his pocket, and hurried down the street. "I have an uneasy feeling about this," he told himself as he entered the bank. "I hope Joe hasn't been fooled."

He laid the passbook and withdrawal form on a teller's counter. When the clerk looked up and recognized Frank, he lifted his eyebrows.

"How do you want this?" he asked.

"In twenty-dollar bills," Frank said. "And please make a record of the serial numbers."

The teller glanced at Frank with a smile. "This is a departure from your usual mysteries, isn't it, Frank? Normally you're on the collecting end instead of the payoff end."

Frank nodded. The teller made a list of the serial numbers and gave the boy a duplicate. Then he stamped the passbook and handed Frank the money. As he started home, Frank remembered the night he had been attacked and kidnapped on this way to the ball park. With such a large sum of money on his person he did not want to take the risk of being held up.

He stopped at headquarters and asked Chief

Collig for a police escort. He was tempted to tell Collig about his suspicions, but decided this might embarrass the Mortons. It would be better to call upon Biff and Tony to carry out the next part of his plan.

After being driven home in a police car, Frank telephoned Biff and Tony. He asked them to drive at once to the road that led past the Morton farm. When Chet and Joe left there, they were to warn the boys if anyone followed them. In any case, Biff and Tony were to keep an eye on Chet until he got home again.

The boys readily agreed. Tony said he would start at once and pick up Biff.

To Frank, the next half-hour ticked by as if every second were a day. He breathed a sigh of relief when the stutter of Chet's jalopy told him the boy was only a block away. Frank rushed to the curb, the envelope with the money in his pocket.

The car made its way erratically down the street, weaving as if the driver were not in full control of his faculties. Chet stopped the car and stared at Frank as if he had never seen him before. His round, full face was damp with perspiration, and his eyes revealed a terrible fear that made his hands tremble on the wheel.

"What's the matter, Chet? Is the trouble bad?" Frank asked. "Come inside and we'll talk it over."

"No—no," Chet pleaded. "Give me the money and let me get back home as quick as I can."

"Where's Joe?"

Chet did not reply for a second, then he whispered, "He—he's coming."

"Can't you stop in for a minute? I'd like to ask you a few questions."

Chet's double chin quivered as he gulped. His mouth was so dry he could hardly rasp out, "Please, please, Frank. No. No. I tell you I have to go. Give me the money."

When Frank drew the envelope from his pocket, Chet snatched it from his hand.

"Chet, you . . ."

"Good-by!" the frightened boy fairly squealed.

The old car lurched forward and rumbled down the street.

As he entered the house again, Frank realized that Chet must be in a state of shock brought about by severe worry. How serious was the Morton trouble? Maybe Joe would be able to tell him when he came.

After twenty minutes went by and his brother still had not returned, Frank became anxious.

"I'll phone the farm," he decided. Mrs. Morton answered.

"This is Frank. Is Joe there?"

"Why, no," was the reply. "I haven't seen him."

"Is Chet home yet?"

"No."

"Well, he has the money," Frank said.

"Money?" Mrs. Morton's voice sounded casual.

"The money you asked for. I gave it to Chet."

There was silence for a moment. "I don't understand, Frank. I didn't ask for any money."

The boy groaned. His hunch had been right. What he had suspected might be a swindle had turned out to be one. What a fool he had been!

And what had happened to Chet and Joe?

CHAPTER XVI

Two Knockouts

SINCE Mrs. Morton knew nothing about the strange request for two thousand five hundred dollars, Frank decided he had better not alarm her before investigating further. Drawing a deep breath, he said:

"When you see Chet and Joe, will you have them get in touch with me right away, Mrs. Morton?"

"Yes, Frank. But what about the money?"

"Chet can explain that better than I can," Frank replied. He said good-by and hung up.

Mrs. Hardy overheard the conversation and immediately became alarmed, even though Frank tried to reassure her.

"Oh, why didn't I listen to you? I've been so gullible," she said tearfully.

Frank's next move was to contact Biff and Tony. Frank's hands were moist with anxiety as he dialed Biff's home. The lanky boy answered.

"Hi, Frank!" he said. "We tailed Chet. Everything's okay."

"But Chet hasn't arrived home."

"Sure he did," Biff insisted. "We saw him drive into his lane."

"Did you watch him go into the house?"

Biff admitted he had not, and at no time had he seen Joe. He and Tony had followed the jalopy to within a block of the Hardy home, he said. They had waited on a side street until Chet began his homeward trip. Then they had followed the rickety car until the stout boy had turned into his driveway, whereupon they had driven back to Bayport.

"Did you see Joe's car anywhere?"

"No."

Before Biff could say more, the telephone operator cut in. "There's an urgent call for Mr. Frank Hardy," she said.

"I'll take it," Frank said, his heart beating faster.

No sooner had Biff hung up than Mrs. Morton's voice said excitedly, "Frank, something awful has happened to Chet."

"What!"

"A neighbor carried him in—unconscious. He was lying alongside the driveway by his car. I just called our doctor!"

"I'll be right out there, Mrs. Morton!"

Frank stopped only long enough to tell his

mother where he was going and to phone for a taxi.

A little while later he was bounding up the farmhouse steps. Chet's mother met him at the door, her face pale with anxiety.

"He's on the sofa," she said, leading the way. "Oh, I wish the doctor would get here!"

Frank looked at his friend. Chet's face was as white as the damp cloth that lay on his forehead. Beneath the compress could be seen the outline of a bump the size of an egg.

"He received an awful blow," Mrs. Morton said.

Frank knelt beside his friend. "Who hit you, Chet?"

The reply was a string of jumbled words. As Frank listened, he began to realize the stark truth of the situation. Quickly he searched Chet's pockets. The envelope with the money was gone!

At that moment the tires of a car sounded in the driveway. Dr. Brown hurried in. As he set his black bag on a chair and began his examination of Chet, the worrisome thought that maybe Joe also had met with foul play prompted Frank to hurry outside.

Catching sight of the Hardy convertible parked next to the Mortons' barn, he ran toward it. Joe was not in the car. Just as Frank was wondering where to look next, he heard a low moan. It seemed to come from the barn.

Quickly he pushed open the sliding door and snapped on a light, almost stumbling over a prone figure as he did so. It was his brother, tied hand and foot, and barely conscious. A thin stream of blood trickled down one side of his face from a wound above the temple.

After ripping open Joe's collar and untying his bonds, Frank revived the semiconscious boy. As Joe struggled to a sitting position, he pressed a hand to his head.

"Ow!" he said. "I can still feel that pistol butt. Where's Chet?"

Frank told him. "And the doctor had better look at you, too, ' he said.

"I'll be all right," Joe said, getting up.

As the boys walked slowly from the barn, Joe gave an account of his harrowing experience. When he had arrived at the Mortons', a tall masked man with a gun had met him at the door. When Joe had resisted, the masked stranger threatened that if his orders were not carried out, Chet's sister Iola would never return to her home. Joe did not know that Chet had already been told the same story.

"I was helpless," Joe said. "When you called, I wanted to tell the truth, but the man was holding a gun against my ribs."

"How did you get slugged?" Frank queried.

"When Chet left for town, the man wouldn't let me go. I tried to sneak off to our car, but he hit me with his pistol butt. That's all I remember until you found me."

The boys went to the house. They entered the living room just as the doctor finished bandaging Chet's head.

"It's only a bad bruise," he said. "But the boy must be kept quiet. Don't question him until after he has had a complete rest."

Dr. Brown examined Joe's head, pronouncing him all right, but advising a good night's rest. As the physician drove off, two policemen arrived. Mrs. Morton had summoned them. Joe stayed long enough to report all he knew, then the Hardys went home.

When the boys confirmed the loss of the money, their mother was inconsolable. Then, bracing herself, she said she was thankful Joe and Chet were safe.

Frank went to telephone Biff. Tony was there, and the two became greatly disturbed over the news.

"I can't help feeling that we're responsible for botching the whole thing," Biff said woefully.

"Of course you weren't," Frank replied. "Nobody could have figured out what was going to happen. But you can help us by supplying any clues you can think of."

Biff recalled that a car without lights had been parked way off the wrong side of the road a short distance from the Morton farm. Biff and Tony thought it had been empty when they passed it, but perhaps it had not been.

Frank was so excited that he remained awake until two o'clock. The thieves had struck because they could not get their hands on the money at police headquarters. They must be captured before they could strike again!

The first step was to consult his father's operative, Sam Radley. Early the next morning he telephoned the man at his hotel.

"Frank," Radley said, after hearing the whole story, "this is a mighty serious case. Assault and battery are bad enough, not to mention grand larceny. We'll go into this thoroughly. I'll be ready to leave here in an hour."

The boys picked him up and they drove to the spot where the empty car had stood.

"Say, Joe," Frank said, "do these tire prints mean anything to you?"

Joe bent down to examine them. "I'll say they do. Same kind as the car that followed the Morton truck after it had been stolen."

"We'll look for more clues," said Sam Radley, pulling a detective's field kit from his pocket.

Using a magnifying glass and tape measure, he went over every inch of the ground and nearby bushes, gathering up samples of dirt onto laboratory slides. Next he went to work on an analysis of what he had found. It was not long before he said:

"All set, fellows. I think we know whom to look for: Two men. One tall, with reddish hair."

"That blasts my idea it was the fake salesman with the blond hair," Joe remarked.

"The other man was short and has an uneven gait," Radley went on. "The red-haired fellow drove the car, which is a new blue sedan with a scratch on the driver's door."

"Wow!" Joe exclaimed. "How did you figure all that, Sam?"

"I simply translated some clues I found," he said, his eyes twinkling.

"Let's have them."

"We know the driver was red-haired because I found two of his hairs on a branch of those hazel bushes which brushed against the door where he stepped out of the car. Also, his stride was long, which means he's tall. The other man's footprints were short and uneven. The impressions made by one of the feet is deeper than the other. He has a slight limp."

"The man who left the letter at the *News* office!" Joe exclaimed.

"How do you know all that about the car?" Frank asked.

"Well, I measured the wheel base and there are some exhaust stains on the grass. The two figures give me the size. I found blue paint flecks under where the driver's door would have been, and on a broken-off twig, which means there's probably a scratch on the car door. So there it is."

"The driver was the tall fellow who put Chet and me out of the picture," Joe surmised.

"We'll see Chet next," the detective said.

"I hope he's awake and can talk," said Frank.

When they entered the Morton home, they found Chet wide awake, lying on the living-room sofa. He had a large tray of lunch on a chair beside him.

"Chet's coming along fine," Mrs. Morton said with a laugh. "Whenever his appetite returns, I know he's well."

The Hardys and Sam Radley began to fire questions at the boy. They learned from him that the tall man had come to the house when Chet was alone, and at gunpoint had forced the defenseless youth to carry out the extortion scheme. The man had hoped to get both Frank and Joe to the farm, but when Frank had stayed home, the thief had changed his plan of attack.

"He told me I'd be followed every minute," Chet said. "One of his pals was hiding in the trunk of the jalopy when I drove to your home. He said he'd shoot me if I went inside the house, or told you anything.

"When I got back here," Chet went on, "somebody jumped from a bush in our driveway and hit me."

"Do you know what the man in your jalopy looked like?" Sam Radley asked.

"No."

"All right. I'll call the police and tell them what happened. They can put out an alert for the two men and the sedan." With that, Radley went to the telephone.

Frank continued to question Chet. "Think hard, Chet! Didn't you get any clue at all?"

"Well, maybe I did. Just when I was seeing stars, I heard someone say, 'The take-off's tomorrow at eleven.' "

Joe glanced at his watch. "It's ten-thirty now!" he exclaimed.

CHAPTER XVII

Trouble at Sea

THE Hardys immediately recalled the incident of the missing Jack Wayne and his plane. Were Chet and Joe's attackers in some way connected with the hijacker?

Joe telephoned the local airport and spoke to a man there who knew the Hardys. The boy suggested that all pilots flying out at eleven be on guard against trouble. He also asked if there were any strangers in a private plane waiting to take off.

"There's no flight scheduled out of here at eleven, either commercial or private," he was told.

Joe contacted the two other nearby airports. A jetliner was leaving from the second, and every precaution would be taken. The Hardys waited at the Morton farm until noon, but no incident was reported from either field.

"Probably the message meant eleven o'clock tonight," Frank said, and called the airports again to renew the warning.

As the afternoon wore on and Mr. Hardy did not return, the boys gave up the idea of going to North Woods that day.

"What say we drive to the airports and do a little checking?" Frank suggested. Everything, however, was routine at the public airports. Nothing had been heard from Wayne or of his plane. And no ship had been chartered for a flight that evening. The boys came away disappointed.

By dinnertime Frank and Joe had reached the conclusion that if the remark had anything to do with a plane, it must be a private one that would take off at eleven, and probably from a private flying field.

Frank declared, "From what's happened so far —wallet, plane, that yacht blinking its lights off and on, and the wailing siren—I believe there might be something doing over the ocean. Suppose we wait out there tonight to find out."

Joe agreed. After dinner the boys told their mother and aunt of the proposed trip. Before Mrs. Hardy could express herself on the subject, Aunt Gertrude said excitedly:

"Take your two-way radio and keep in touch. If anybody bothers you, I'll give him a piece of my mind!"

The boys promised to take the set. Reluctantly Mrs. Hardy agreed to their going. Just before dark, they left for their boathouse, carrying binoculars as well as the radio. Joe unloosed the moorings and they shoved off.

The motor purred into action, but the young detectives decided on a trial spin before heading toward the open sea.

"She's okay," Frank called, after the boys had circled the bay a few times.

He guided the motorboat out of the inlet, which they had negotiated so perilously the evening of the storm. Tonight the ocean was as smooth as a new highway. Stars twinkled in the cloudless sky, but there was little light from the thin crescent moon.

"Oh, oh," Joe said presently. "We'd better not forget Aunt Gertrude." He pulled up the collapsible antenna and switched on the two-way radio. "Hello, Aunt Gertrude. Are you listening?" Then he turned the selector to hear her answer.

The receiver crackled with static, which was followed by a voice like an umpire calling a strike. "Listening! I've been waiting an hour. Where are you boys?"

"On a calm sea. Nothing to worry about."

The boys did not know whether what they heard was static or Aunt Gertrude snorting.

As Joe clicked off the set, he heard another motorboat and glanced back. He noticed moving red and green lights not far away.

"I'm afraid we're being followed!" he said to his brother.

Frank peered across their churning wake. The strange boat was gaining rapidly on them. He let out the throttle all the way, and the *Sleuth* leaped forward like a frightened rabbit.

For a few minutes it seemed as if it were putting distance between the two crafts. But the space gradually diminished. Joe turned on the radio.

"Aunt Gertrude, we think we're being followed by another boat. It's overtaking us. I'm going to hide the radio until we find out what's going on. Let you know later what happens."

He had barely collapsed the aerial and secreted the radio when the prow of a powerful speedboat pulled alongside them. Two men were in it.

"Stop!" one of them shouted.

Frank tried to get a good look at the strangers, but both of them wore hats pulled down low and collars turned up.

One of the men grabbed the side of the *Sleuth* and beamed a flashlight on the name plate. "Turn around and go back!" he commanded sharply.

"What for?" Joe said cheerfully. "Can't a couple of fellows have some fun?"

"You guys can have some fun ashore," the man sneered. "Do what I tell you, or else!"

"We're just out for a spin," Frank said as light-heartedly as he could under the conditions. "But we don't like being ordered to go home. Who are you, anyway?"

"It's not for kids to ask questions," said the man, vaulting into the *Sleuth*.

He was several inches over six feet and as burly as a bear. Menacingly he approached Joe.

"Are you going to scram?"

"No."

The man lunged at Joe, who tried to grapple with him. Frank sprang to his brother's defense, but before he could clamp a hold on the stranger, the assailant had pitched Joe far over the side of the boat. After a brief struggle Frank followed. The Hardys bobbed to the surface several feet from the boats.

Frank hissed into Joe's ear, "Pretend we can't swim."

The boys thrashed about madly, crying for help.

As the big man leaped back into his own boat, Joe heard him laugh and shout to his companion:

"That sure was easy. Let's go and report to the boss."

"Shall we take their boat in tow?" asked the other.

"The tide'll take care of that, pal," the big man shouted. "We've done what we were ordered to do. Let's scram!"

Frank and Joe forced themselves beneath the

surface of the water several times, giving a genuine appearance of drowning. When the men saw this, they gave satisfied grunts and sped off.

By this time the lights of the bobbing *Sleuth* were farther away.

"We'll really have to swim for it," Frank said.

With steady, powerful strokes, the Hardys made for their drifting boat. They reached it together and hauled themselves over the side. Tumbling into the bottom, they lay still for a moment to catch their breath.

"We'd better turn off our lights," Frank said, reaching for the switch.

After everything had been quiet for several minutes, Joe reached for the radio and turned on the sender. In a hoarse whisper he said, "Aunt Gertrude, are you still there?"

"Yes," came the answer. "Frank! Joe! Are you all right?"

When her nephew reported what had happened, Miss Hardy gasped.

"I knew something would happen. I was just about to send the police launch. Did those pirates leave?"

"Yes. We fooled 'em. As soon as we're sure they can't hear our engine, we're going farther out," Joe said, and switched off the set.

A few minutes later Frank started the motor and guided the *Sleuth* into deeper water. Not a ship was in sight, but a few minutes later they could just make out twinkling lights in the distance.

Joe pulled out the binoculars he had brought along. "It looks like the yacht we saw the night of the storm," he reported. "Listen!"

A siren was wailing! Its hollow, mournful sound crescendoed and wailed across the ocean.

Just as suddenly came the roar of a helicopter. Frank and Joe glanced at the *Sleuth*'s clock. It was eleven-fifteen.

As the boys listened, the sound of the helicopter grew louder. The Hardys peered into the sky but could not see anything. Apparently the craft was traveling without lights.

"The same setup as the other night!" Frank cried excitedly.

"I see it!" Joe shouted.

The rotor blades twirled lazily as the craft came lower and lower.

"We'd better scram!" Joe cried out.

Frank was about to turn the *Sleuth* when the siren wailed again. To the boys' relief the helicopter moved off.

"I'll bet that was a signal," Frank said. "Do you suppose that ship . . . ?"

His question went unfinished as a flash of light came from the direction of the yacht. Then darkness again.

The helicopter was edging off in the direction of the ship. "That must have been a signal flare!"

"Let's go closer. I'll tell Aunt Gertrude what's going on," Joe said.

By mistake he clicked the receiving switch. Suddenly Miss Hardy's voice crackled over the radio.

"Boys, are you there? I have an important message—"

Joe switched to the sender. "Yes, we're here. Something's doing."

"Well, leave it and come home. Your father is back in town and wants you."

"We can't come now."

"There's been a burglary at a factory. Part of the money stolen from Chet was found there."

"Switch that off!" Frank commanded as he cut the *Sleuth*'s motor.

He had observed a launch speeding toward them from the direction of the yacht.

"If it's those same men, we're sunk this time," Joe said, hiding the radio once again.

The boys counted on the darkness to conceal the *Sleuth*. There was a bright light on the yacht now. The helicopter was directly over it. A wire ladder dangled from the chopper. A man was descending it.

"Great crow!" Joe exclaimed. "I'll bet the wallet we found was dropped from that helicopter!"

"Get down!" Frank warned as Joe craned his neck to see better.

He ducked to the floor of the *Sleuth* just as the launch's searchlight swept across it. Before it swung back, the Hardys had covered themselves with tarpaulin to avoid detection. The light was trained steadily on the *Sleuth* as the other boat rushed toward it.

There came the sound of a loud splash. It was followed by a string of oaths from the boat, which was now almost beside the *Sleuth.*

A muffled voice from the boat gave them a clue. "There goes five thousand dollars. The boss'll pin somebody's ears back for this."

"For ten grand I wouldn't be in that guy's shoes," came a gruff reply. "Bad enough to lose that wallet. Well, let's take a look at that boat."

Through a crack in the tarpaulin Joe could see that the rays of the launch's searchlight were probing every corner of the *Sleuth* for signs of life.

"Just a driftin' boat. Prob'ly the one those kids had who got drowned. Yep, this is it—the *Sleuth.*"

At that moment a wailing sound filled the air.

"There's the siren," the gruff voice said. "We ain't got much time."

"I'm goin' to hop in and take a look, anyhow," the persistent fellow replied. "I might find somethin' worth takin'."

"I ain't so sure. Last time we hit port, Renny—"

"Shut up! I'm goin' to take a look."

The Hardys felt the *Sleuth* lurch as one of the men leaped over the side.

The boys held their breath, fearful that even the pounding of their hearts might be heard.

"Hey! I found a radio—one of them two-way jobs," the man said. "I'll see if it works."

He clicked it on. The next instant a woman's voice cried out clearly:

"This is Aunt Gertrude. Frank and Joe Hardy, why don't you answer me? Do you need any help?"

The man shut the set off and gave a low laugh. "Well, Mr. Hardy, tell Aunt Gertrude for me they've gone to Davy Jones's locker."

There was a loud, coarse guffaw. "Bring that radio! Maybe we'll hear something from the big dick himself. He's getting too hot."

The man handed the radio across the water. The *Sleuth* swayed as he took a long step backward. His foot planted itself squarely upon Frank's back!

CHAPTER XVIII

Caught!

INSTINCTIVELY Frank let out a stifled gasp as the intruder's heel dug into his ribs.

The tarpaulin covering was ripped off. A hairy sailor towered over him.

"Ha!" the man shouted in anger. "One of the Hardy boys! Jeff was wrong. You didn't drown!"

He reached down, grasped Frank's shirt front, and pulled the boy to his feet.

"I'll knock you cold before I toss you over. Then you won't never come back to life!" he threatened.

Frank watched. As the big fellow cocked his arm, the youth caught a glimpse of Joe peeling off the canvas covering and rising behind the burly thug.

The man in the launch saw the move, too. "There's another kid!" he shouted.

His warning came too late. Before the hamlike

fist could start its forward journey, Frank, with the agility of a tiger, delivered a shove to his assailant's mid-section. As the man teetered, Joe flung a crushing body block against the back of his legs.

The sailor keeled over like a falling tree, his head cracking against the gunwale. He rolled over on his face, moaned, and lay still on the bottom of the *Sleuth*.

So swiftly had the blow been struck that the man in the launch stared, speechless. He reached toward the dashboard and pressed a button. Then, letting out a shrill yell, he made a flying leap for the Hardys. He landed in the *Sleuth* simultaneously with a rumbling noise that quickly rose to a wail.

"He's set off a siren!" Joe cried out.

Frank plunged into the fellow, knocking him on top of his henchman. Joe flung himself into the melee, and together the boys pinned him down.

Above the din they heard another siren. "The yacht's answering!" Frank cried.

The prisoner beneath the boys snarled and puffed.

"Save your strength," Frank retorted. "You'll need it for the swim back."

"Let's tie him up and take him with us," Joe suggested. "That'll make two prisoners who may be able to help us solve the riddle of the wailing siren."

"No." Frank said. "Carrying both of them will

make too much weight for the *Sleuth*. We're going to have to run for it and we'll need every bit of speed. I think our one prisoner will tell plenty."

From across the water a speedboat churned rapidly in their direction.

"Here you go, sailor!" Frank said.

The boys lifted the struggling man over the side of the *Sleuth*. He hit the water with a flat splash. Spluttering, he started swimming toward the launch, which had drifted some yards away.

Instantly Joe took the wheel and started the *Sleuth*'s engine. As it leaped into action, Frank yanked a life jacket from a locker. Bending over their prisoner, he thrust the man's limp arms into it and buckled the straps.

"What are you doing?" Joe shouted.

"This fellow may have to be our secret weapon," Frank replied.

"How?"

Before Frank could explain, the searchlight from the launch suddenly started to move across the water. The sailor had reached his own boat, climbed in, and was after them!

"Great crow!" Joe exclaimed. "We can't make it, Frank, with two boats after us!"

"Don't be too sure."

Frank kept a wary eye on the unconscious man beside him, at the same time listening to the racing motor of the *Sleuth*. His insistence upon perfection in its engine was paying dividends. Joe made a beeline for the inlet. Although they were outdistancing the launch, the speedboat was creeping up. Suddenly there was a shot.

"They're firing on us!" Joe shouted.

Their prisoner began to revive. He twisted from side to side, mumbling. Frank could catch nothing intelligible. It sounded like *crack—gun —crack.*

Frank watched the man carefully to remain master of the situation. He felt in the captive's pockets for weapons, or something that might identify him with the gang of smugglers or kidnappers. He found nothing.

"If the guy in the speedboat gets too close, I'm going to turn around and ram him!" Joe cried.

"You won't have to."

"How the dickens are we going to beat him? Look at him gain on us!"

"There's your answer!" Frank pointed to their prisoner. As the speedboat raced to head off the *Sleuth* before she could make the narrow inlet, he shouted, "Now's the time!"

He helped the life-jacketed man to his feet. "You okay?" he asked.

"Sure. Why—?" The sailor suddenly realized what was about to happen. His fist shot out.

But Frank was ready for him. He dodged, caught the sailor off balance, and pushed him into the sea.

"Now's our chance!" he shouted. "Run for it, Joe!"

Over the roar of the motor the boys heard a shout. Immediately the speedboat throttled down and came alongside the swimming sailor. At the same moment, the launch made a quick turn and barely avoided running down the man in the water. The boys could hear the engine going into reverse.

Joe urged the *Sleuth* to its top speed and grinned at his brother. "Your secret weapon worked swell!"

But the man in the launch did not give up the chase. After standing by to see that the sailor was picked up, he renewed the pursuit. The gun went into action again, and the boys crouched low. Bullet after bullet sang over their heads or spat into the waves. Joe was zigzagging the *Sleuth*'s course.

"He's really pouring it on," Joe said grimly.

"Gosh, if we only had our radio, Joe, we could have told Aunt Gertrude to notify the Coast Guard."

Again the launch was gaining on them. The speedboat had turned back toward the dim hulk of the yacht.

"If we can only make the bay," Frank thought, "I know of plenty of places to hide where the water's shallow and that launch can't follow us."

"Here—we—are!" Joe shouted.

He applied a stiff left rudder. The *Sleuth* took

the turn like a champion and sped through the mouth of Barmet Bay.

A snug cove lay a quarter of a mile ahead. The racing *Sleuth* reached it and turned in. There was no sign of the pursuing launch.

"We lost them!" Joe cried in relief. "I thought they had us! Too bad about our prisoner. He might have told us plenty."

"He didn't have a thing in his pockets," said Frank. "And besides, he probably wouldn't have talked. We'd better phone the Coast Guard pronto."

Joe docked at an all-night waterfront restaurant in the inlet. Frank jumped out and rushed for a pay phone. When he had finished his detailed report, the lieutenant said, "We'll dispatch a boat at once to look for the speedboat and the launch. And I'll notify our stations along the coast to go after that yacht and also check on the helicopter. I'll get in touch with Police Chief Collig too."

A few minutes later Joe guided the *Sleuth* to their boathouse. When the brothers arrived home, the Hardy house was brightly lighted and alive with excitement.

"It's you! Thank goodness!" Aunt Gertrude exclaimed.

Briefly Frank and Joe told what had happened to them. In turn they asked for particulars about the burglars at the factory, and whether their father had reported anything further.

"No," Mrs. Hardy answered. "You're to stand by until he calls. In the meantime you'd better get to bed."

As the boys were putting on pajamas a little later, Frank said he thought the house should be guarded.

"That gang may still try something desperate —and before morning." He slipped into slacks and moccasins. "I'm going downstairs," he said.

"I'll take a turn later," Joe told him. "But call me if you hear anything."

It was nearly two o'clock when Frank halted at a side window that looked out on the driveway. As he peered through the narrow space, he drew back quickly. Was it an illusion, or did he detect a motion in the bushes beside the garage?

Every muscle in the boy's body tensed as he watched. The bushes parted and a man looked out. The dark figure stood motionless as if to listen, then made a "come-on" motion with his hand. Immediately the bushes parted again and a second figure emerged from the shadows. Together they tiptoed toward the house, hugging the shadows.

Frank raced upstairs to summon Joe. The younger boy, rousing instantly, hopped into slacks and loafers and hastened to the first floor.

"There they are!" Frank whispered, pointing to the space below the shade of the side window "They're coming to the back door."

"They can't open it."

"I unlocked it. We'll jump 'em."

"Good strategy."

The boys tiptoed into the kitchen and stood behind the door. Soon they heard a low voice say:

"We can't fail this time. We've got to get Hardy's reports . . ."

"We'll try the door, then one of the windows." The knob turned. "What do you know? They left this door unlocked."

The door opened slowly.

"Okay!" came a hoarse whisper. "This way. Don't make a sound. And watch out for the two boys."

As a dark figure appeared in the doorway, Joe charged like a young bull, hitting the intruder a solid blow and tumbling him onto the porch.

Frank followed with a flying tackle in the direction of the second man, but missed him. He dashed off through the yard and vaulted the hedge. Frank went after him.

Joe was still grappling with the man on the porch. The struggling prisoner suddenly jackknifed his knees and was about to deliver a vicious kick at the boy's head when the porch light went on and a voice shouted:

"Don't you dare!"

A rush of footsteps was instantly followed by a sharp blow, and the man went limp as an empty glove. Joe jumped up.

Joe charged like a young bull

The light from the kitchen revealed Aunt Gertrude, her brother's hickory stick in her right hand, standing over the prone figure.

"Try to harm my nephew, will you?" she said, waving the cane menacingly.

As the man moaned and tried to sit up, Joe gasped. The fellow was tall and had red hair!

"You!" the boy cried out. "The man who knocked out my friend Chet and me and took our two thousand dollars!"

The prisoner glared. "I don't know what you're talkin' about," he muttered weakly.

"Oh, yes, you do," Joe said. Aunt Gertrude handed him a rope and he bound the intruder's arms and legs. "You're one of the gang my father's after. You're smuggling rifles out of this country."

For an instant there was a look of guilty surprise on the man's face, then he denied ever having heard of such a thing.

By this time Mrs. Hardy had arrived on the scene, and suggested they go inside the house.

"This is all a mistake, lady!" the prisoner pleaded.

"We'll let the police decide that."

Before they could telephone headquarters, Frank came rushing into the house. "You've got him!" he cried, seeing the prisoner. "That practically proves we have the right car!"

"What car?" Joe asked.

Frank explained that when he chased the red-haired man's companion along the street back of the Hardys', the fellow had started to cross over to a parked car. He had changed his mind when two policemen loomed up beside it, and he had sped on.

"Was he caught?"

"No. He was too quick for Smuff and Riley and me."

"Smuff and Riley?"

Frank nodded. "They were given this beat to patrol, and actually found a blue car with a scratch on the door. It fits the description of the one parked near Chet's farm."

The prisoner's jaw opened in astonishment. Frank went on, "If he won't tell us who he is, the motor vehicle department will."

"It's not my car!" the man cried out. "It belongs to . . ." Suddenly he realized he had said too much, and from then on kept sullenly silent.

"Where are Smuff and Riley?" Aunt Gertrude asked. "Bring them here to take this—this cutthroat away!"

Officer Riley came in, puffing from the exertion of pushing the car around the corner. Smuff was guarding it at the curb.

"A prisoner, eh?" Riley beamed. "You sure got him tied up for delivery." He laughed at his own joke. "Well, I'll take him to headquarters."

"Just a minute," Frank said. "I believe the rest of the gang may have been brought in by the Coast Guard. I'll make a phone call."

He went to the hall telephone and spoke to the lieutenant, first telling him of the red-haired man's capture, then asking if the launch or speedboat or yacht had been boarded.

The officer said his men had returned empty-handed. The suspected craft had too much of a headstart. He assured Frank, however, that a plane would be sent out at daybreak to check on the yacht.

Frank hung up, but stayed at the telephone. In a loud voice he said excitedly, "Oh, that's just great, Lieutenant! Now our prisoner will certainly talk!"

He returned to the kitchen. Continuing his hoax, he said to their captive, "Quite a racket you fellows were carrying on. How did you ever get tangled up in such a dangerous business? Uncle Sam has taken a hand in it now!"

The man glowered, but remained silent.

Both Frank and Joe tried to force a further confession from him, but he remained obdurate. Finally Frank said:

"We may as well turn you over to the police. They have ways of making people talk. Riley, how about calling headquarters for a car to take this guy down?"

"Sure thing, Frank," the officer assented.

"Then I'll go outside and tell Smuff what's happened." He went to the telephone. While he was gone, Joe said:

"I wish we could keep our prisoner here until we hear from Dad."

The man greeted these words with an evil snort.

"Your dad, eh? Fenton Hardy! I knew we'd get around to that."

"What do you mean?"

"Listen here. If you promise to let me go, I might be able to make a little deal with you folks."

"We don't go for deals," Joe said. "But what's on your mind?"

"It's simple. In exchange for my freedom I'll give you some important information. I'll tell you where they're holding your father!"

CHAPTER XIX

Danger in North Woods

"DAD captured?" Joe shouted in disbelief.

The man nodded, smiling evilly. Mrs. Hardy turned white, and Aunt Gertrude put an arm about her.

"How do we know you're not lying?" Joe asked evenly.

The man shrugged. "That's up to you."

The Hardys moved out of earshot of the criminal for a whispered conference. All agreed that the story of the factory theft might have been a means of luring the detective into a trap.

"We'll check on this burglary," Joe said. "Where was it?"

"In Hambleton at the airplane motors factory."

"I'll call the police." Joe hurried upstairs to his father's study. But neither the local nor State Police had heard of the theft. Joe came downstairs and relayed the news to his family.

"I can't believe Dad would walk into a trap that easily," said Frank. "Wait a minute. I want to look for something in his files."

He went to the study and unlocked Fenton Hardy's filing cabinet, which he had permission to do in case of emergency.

Thumbing through the files, Frank noted that Mr. Hardy was under contract to direct plant security work at the Hambleton company where secret government work was being carried on.

The name and private number of the company's president were listed. Frank quickly dialed.

Mr. Hartwick answered. When Frank had convinced him of his identity, Mr. Hartwick said:

"Yes, Frank. There has been a burglary here. We're keeping it secret to tackle the problem from the inside first."

"Is Dad all right?"

"Yes, so far as I know. He's out here now."

"Will you find him and have him phone home? Something important has come up here."

As Frank hurried down the stairs he heard scuffling in the kitchen. The redheaded man was trying desperately to get away.

"Your trick didn't work," Frank announced. "I know where my father is."

Frank told the others that Mr. Hardy was safe. Just then the telephone rang. Moments later Frank heard the calm voice of his father at the other end of the line.

Frank quickly told all that had happened to them on the ocean and later. Fenton Hardy listened in amazement. When the boy had finished, the detective said:

"You boys have done a great job. Now there are two things I want you to do. Try to find out something about the helicopter. And meet me here at noon."

"Yes, Dad."

As Frank said good-by, a prowl car stopped in front of the house. Two policemen jumped out and hustled the prisoner into the car.

The Hardy home became quiet once more as the four occupants retired for some much-needed sleep. Frank and Joe did not awaken until nine o'clock. As soon as they were dressed, Joe telephoned the Coast Guard. After a long conversation he hung up.

"The Coast Guard's flying boat located the yacht," he told Frank.

"Did they stop it?"

"Landed alongside and boarded her."

"What did they find?"

"Nothing! Everything was in order and the captain, named Haxon, denied any connection with a helicopter. If the yacht was carrying smuggled goods, the captain probably got scared and ordered it dumped overboard. Anyway, the plane's keeping an eye on the yacht as she goes down the coast."

A desperate effort to find a trace of the helicopter drew a blank.

"It's a private helicopter—very private," Joe concluded. "And flies only at night. But we'll find it, just as soon as this burglary business is settled."

At eleven-thirty the boys started out to meet their father. The factory was surrounded by a high wire fence. As Frank drove up to the main gate, he was stopped by a uniformed guard.

The guard studied the boys' identifications for a moment. "Okay," he said. "We've been waiting for you."

The brothers were soon ushered into Mr. Hartwick's office. Their father and the company president were seated at a desk, minutely examining something with a magnifying glass.

"Hello, boys," the detective greeted them. "Mr. Hartwick, I want you to meet Frank and Joe, my two assistants."

The boys shook hands with him, and the detective continued. "Burglars broke into this plant last night and stole a quantity of secret airplane gadgets being made for use in United States military planes. As they left, one of them dropped this."

He held up a twenty-dollar bill. "Ever see this before?" He handed the money over.

Frank looked at the serial number, comparing it with the list in his wallet. "I'll say so! This is one of the bills I gave to Chet."

"Just as I figured," the detective said. "Either the extortionists and the burglars are the same people, or they're associated in some way. Boys, I want you to do something for me."

"Yes, Dad?"

"Tour this plant as if you were on an inspection trip of some kind. Keep your eyes open for that phony salesman you saw at Chet's farm, or anybody else you've caught a glimpse of in this mystery. We think one or more of the gang we're after may be working right here."

Guided by a junior executive, the boys went from one department to another, but nobody answered the description of any of the suspects. Frank and Joe were completing the tour in the packing department when Joe stopped short and pointed.

"Frank, look at that engine over there!"

"That's just like the one we saw in the shack in the woods!" his brother said in a low voice.

The boys hastened back to their father and voiced their suspicions. The detective looked at Mr. Hartwick. "Have you missed any motors?"

"Several," Mr. Hartwick replied. "But we thought they were lost by the trucking company. We've sent through a tracer but haven't heard a thing yet."

The Hardys were convinced the motors had been stolen and hidden in North Woods.

"We won't put off our trip to the woods any

longer," the boys' father said. "I only hope those suspects haven't moved out."

The company president thanked the Hardys for their help and they left the factory. They arrived home to find Aunt Gertrude standing on the front steps, an envelope in her hands.

"A state trooper brought this a second ago," she said. "It's for you, Fenton."

Mr. Hardy opened the envelope, his eyes taking on a look of satisfaction as he read the enclosure. "Even better than I thought," he said, explaining that he had asked for a list of any recent factory thefts along the Atlantic seaboard. "This note says there have been thefts in five airplane and three rifle manufacturing plants. The thing to do now is fit the pieces of this puzzle together."

After a hasty luncheon, Mr. Hardy asked his sons to come to his study. Reaching into his gun case, he pulled out two pistols.

"Take these. You may need them if the wolves attack. I'll make out the appropriate permits for you to carry them. We're on a dangerous mission."

"Dad, do you think these thefts of airplane parts and rifles are tied up with the mystery of the wailing siren?" Frank asked.

"Yes. I'm sure they're being shipped out of the country on that yacht."

"With the help of the helicopter?" Joe asked excitedly.

"That's what we have to prove. It may be a difficult matter to locate the helicopter. But the clues you boys have picked up seem to tie together neatly," Mr. Hardy said admiringly.

He checked his own pistol, then picked up a peculiar-looking weapon, which he put into a shoulder holster.

"This is a special gun," he said. "It doesn't kill —just shoots a gas that acts as an anesthetic."

With admonitions from Mrs. Hardy and Aunt Gertrude to be careful, the three hurried to the boys' car. Frank took the wheel and drove to the trail which the campers had taken. With Joe in the lead, they started off through the woods.

Upon reaching the brook, they crossed it and went in a straight line toward the wolf-man's cabin.

The Hardys pressed quickly and silently through the dense woodland for half an hour. Suddenly they became aware of distant howls.

"The wolves!" Joe said.

"They've picked up our scent!" Frank cried out.

The boys loaded their pistols. Mr. Hardy led the way, halting suddenly behind a thorny bush.

"The wire stockade!" Joe whispered.

Before them was the enclosure, from which came the howling of the excited wolves.

Mr. Hardy took out his shoulder gun. "Temporary sleep won't harm these beasts!" he said.

"While I'm giving them a taste of this gas, you boys see if their owner's at home and keep him busy till I show up."

As the detective crept forward through the heavy brush, Frank and Joe angled off in the direction of the cabin. When they had almost reached it, they halted.

Before them, framed in the dark doorway, stood the bearded wolf-man. He stepped out, quickly followed by another man, who was small, stooped, and unshaven. When they saw the boys, both men stopped short.

"I thought I told you trespassers to stay away from here!" the wolves' owner shouted at them angrily.

"We'd like to talk to you," Frank said.

The smaller man grinned at his companion through two broken teeth. "Who are they, Krack? Friends of yours?"

Krack! Another piece of the puzzle suddenly dropped into place. The man from the launch had mumbled *Krack—gun—Krack!*

"The only things that talk around here are the wolves," Krack said cuttingly. He motioned with his hand. "Come here, Saber!"

At his command, the wolf stalked through the doorway. It eyed the boys savagely, whining for his master to give the word and he would be at their throats.

The boys thrust their hands into their pockets.

The pistols were ready. They would use them only in case . . .

Suddenly Saber pricked up his ears. Krack took notice.

"There's somebody at the stockade, Jezro!" he cried out. Then he bellowed at the wolf. "Stockade, Saber! Kill!"

Gooseflesh rose on the Hardy boys as the brute dashed toward the stockade. They had forgotten to warn their father about this killer!

CHAPTER XX

A Surprise Capture

THE Hardy boys stared in horror as the wolf bounded toward the stockade.

They raced after it, pistols poised to shoot if they could sight the animal. Suddenly, from near the cage, came the report of a gun. There was a yelp of pain, then complete silence.

When Frank and Joe reached the clearing, their father was not in sight. The caged wolves lay in a stupor. Saber was dead.

Krack and Jezro arrived on the heels of the boys. They stared transfixed at the sight. Then Jezro gave a crazy laugh and dashed off among the trees.

"Come back here!" Krack cried out.

"I'm gettin' out of here and you've got no wolves to stop me!" Jezro flung back.

A bullet from Krack's gun hissed through the trees.

"We'd better go before he aims that thing at us," Frank advised. "He'll get wise in a minute that we're mixed up in this."

"You bet. Let's follow Jezro. Maybe he'll spill what he knows."

Out of range of Krack, Frank and Joe took off after Jezro. The man's speed proved no match for the fleet-footed Hardys.

Joe leaped upon his back, bringing the scrawny man to the ground. Frank collared him and raised the fugitive to a sitting position.

"Lemme go!" he whined. "Maybe them wolves ain't dead."

"I can guarantee they'll take a long sleep," Frank said. "Now, what's going on here?"

Jezro remained silent.

"All right. If you won't talk, we'll tell you a few things. You stole a truck with rifles and hardware and camping equipment, and brought it here."

"No, I didn't. It was Red Mike. He's daffy over campin' stuff. I never leave these woods."

"Does your friend Mike have red hair?" Frank asked.

"Yeah. How'd you know?"

"We caught him. He's in jail."

Now thoroughly frightened, Jezro told the boys he was a wanted thief, who had met Krack while hiding out in the tumble-down shack in the woods.

"He got me to work with him and his friends,"

Jezro said. "Promised me big money to help 'em keep people out o' the woods."

"Where were you when we came to the woods before?" Joe prodded him.

"Following you. I was spyin' on you when you found Mike's canoe."

"Our canoe," Frank corrected. "Go on."

"Mike and Trippek were in Wells Hardware buying a new fish pole the day your fat friend was there," Jezro said. "That boy sure was giving everybody an earful about his uncle's rifles. So right then and there Mike decided to swipe the truck and take everything in it."

"Who's Trippek?" Frank interrupted.

"Tall, blond fellow."

"Sells insect repellent?"

"He did once so he could find out about you fellows. Then I watched you guys when you came here. I marked those trees to make the trail." He laughed. "It got you out of the way, easy enough "

"I suppose you dug the pit to trap us," Frank said.

"No Krack did. He didn't want nobody prowlin' around the woods. Listen here. You ought to let me go. I done you a favor. I left you a note tellin' you it was dangerous here."

Joe gave Frank a wink. "Do you believe that? Crooks hang together. Jezro wouldn't squeal on Krack."

"Oh, wouldn't I? Listen, boys, I'm a thief, but I

don't steal things to help people make war on their own country!"

Before Frank could ask Jezro to explain his startling remark, the sound of a wailing siren filled the woods. Joe looked into the sky, half expecting to see a helicopter.

"That's from the cabin," Jezro said. "Krack's warnin' the other men."

Frank realized that if Krack's henchmen were near, the boys would have to hurry to uncover the loot they were seeking.

"Where are they hiding the stolen stuff, Jezro?" he asked sharply.

"I'll tell you, but you gotta let me go if I do."

"We won't hurt you," Joe said. "But don't try to get away, or it'll go hard with you."

Jezro nodded and led the boys into a thicket. After he had gone a hundred yards he stopped.

"The stuff's hidden in there," he said, pointing to a dense copse.

"I'll take a look," Frank told his brother. "You guard Jezro."

Frank made his way cautiously. Presently he came to an extensive clearing over which was stretched a green canvas with bushes and branches laid here and there upon it. Pulling up one edge of the camouflage, Frank uncovered a row of lights, set along the ground.

"Jeepers!" he exclaimed half-aloud. "A landing field for the helicopter."

The solution to the wailing siren mystery was becoming clear. Stolen plane parts, engines, arms, and ammunition were being hidden in the wilderness. They were picked up by the helicopter at night and carried out to sea, where they were secretly loaded onto the yacht.

"The wailing siren is used to announce its comings and goings," Frank concluded. "I wonder where the helicopter is now."

Frank searched a little longer, but could find none of the equipment stolen from Chet. He hurried back to make Jezro reveal the spot. As he reached him and Joe, he noticed some bushes moving just ahead. Before he could shout a warning, three men, pistols in hand, jumped out of concealment.

"Reach for the clouds!" one of them snapped. He had blond hair and a voice that was familiar. Trippek!

"Frisk 'em, men, and tie 'em up," came an order from a small dark man with a limp. He was Rainy Night, the man who had left the note at the newspaper office and later had helped steal the Hardys' money from Chet.

He turned to Jezro. "As for you, you traitor, you'll get the same treatment."

"Please, Renny, don't do this to me!" Jezro wailed. "I ain't told 'em nothin'."

The dark-haired man sneered. "Think that

over while you're starving to death. You and your two pals here!"

The men pulled several long pieces of wire from their pockets. Standing the Hardys and Jezro against a tree, they bound them fast to the trunk.

Trippek chuckled. "Haxon would get a kick out of this!" he said.

Haxon! Frank and Joe looked at each other. The captain of the yacht!

At that moment Krack came striding out of the woods. He shot a contemptuous glance at Jezro and the boys.

"Please, please," Jezro begged. "I was only foolin'."

"Shut up! I'll deal with you later." Krack turned toward the other men. "Bad luck. That's all we've had since these brats started spying on us."

"Better not talk here," Trippek advised.

Krack jerked a thumb toward the boys. "They're as good as finished, so it won't hurt if they listen in."

"What's up?" Trippek asked, worried.

"The yacht's been boarded. Haxon sent me the message short wave."

"Did they dump the load?"

"Just in time. Haxon said one motor accidentally fell into the ocean from the copter. The Coast Guard, even with the evidence destroyed, will keep an eye on Haxon and the yacht."

"What's the caper now?" one of the others asked.

"To move. I wish we had brought the copter back here."

"Where is it?"

"In the barn at Beekman's farm."

The boys knew the secluded place on the outskirts of North Woods. It had been abandoned a long time and would serve as a perfect hiding place.

"We'll keep Fenton Hardy there until the heat is off," Krack said, looking at the boys.

The boys were startled, but remembering the trick their prisoner Red Mike had tried to play at the Hardy house, Frank said, "You'll not catch Dad."

Krack laughed. "Oh no? We have him now. Caught him near the wolf pen."

"You're bluffing," Joe said.

Krack pulled Mr. Hardy's gas gun from his belt. "Recognize this? If it had another load of gas in it, I'd let you have it."

Perspiration broke out on the boys' foreheads. With their father captured, the outlook appeared bleak indeed. Nevertheless, Joe defiantly reminded Krack that the police would soon catch up with them.

"Thanks for reminding me of the police," Krack said with a sneer. "Men, I'll open the wolves' pen. They'll be awake soon. If the cops come, they'll get theirs. We'll stay in the caves while the wolves take care of 'em."

In the conversation that followed, Frank and Joe learned an amazing story of foreign intrigue which was being conducted by Renny, alias Rainy Night, whose real name was Renaldo. These men were working for a large unscrupulous foreign combine which had planned uprisings in Central America.

From what they could piece together from bits of conversation, the group had been making systematic thefts of American currency. With it they were secretly buying arms, ammunition, and plane parts or bribing dishonest factory workers to steal airplane engines and equipment.

North Woods had been chosen as a base of operations because it was so near the seacoast, yet not likely to be subject to interference. The contraband was crated here before being transported to the yacht by the helicopter.

"So the packing was the hammering we heard on the sound detector," Joe said to Jezro.

Krack overheard the remark. "Yes," he replied, "but our own detector warned us you were gettin' too close, so we stopped work."

Encouraged by Krack's bragging, Frank and Joe shot questions at them. Renaldo, they learned, was a notorious South American racketeer. He had met Krack, an unprincipled animal trainer, in the underworld, and had arranged the North Woods deal with him. Krack, in turn, had found Trippek and the others.

Krack suddenly gave an uproarious laugh. "You kids got the two grand Renny dropped while he was climbing into the helicopter, but we found a way to get it back through that fat friend of yours. We paid off one of our stooges with it."

So that was how the telltale money found its way into the Hambleton plant!

By this time the racketeers, pleased with the impression they thought they were making on the doomed Hardy boys, answered questions freely. It was Krack and Renaldo who had kidnapped Frank and sent the carrier pigeons.

"Where did the first pigeon go?" Joe asked.

"North Carolina," said Krack. "Brother of mine lives there."

"Did you take the other pigeon from our garage?"

Trippek nodded, a pleased grin on his face. He seemed to be aware of the efforts the three Hardys had made to trace the home cote of the pigeons.

"Who was the woman who followed me from the post office?" Frank asked.

"A friend of mine. Good scout, too. She warned Trip when your brother showed up."

"Was Renaldo the one who dropped the dark glasses at our house?" Joe asked.

"Yeah. When he found your father wasn't home, he decided to have one of you two kids snatched."

"Listen here," one of the men in the background called out. "You've told these kids enough now to hang us all."

"They won't be around long," Krack said confidently. "I'll turn out a couple of wolves soon as it's dark. I know that gas they got. Only knocks 'em out a few hours."

The three prisoners shuddered at the thought of being torn to pieces by ravening wild beasts. The sun already had set. In a few hours the woods would be cloaked in darkness, the—

"Come on!" Krack ordered. "Let's get back to the cabin. I'm going to see if I can get a coded message through to Haxon before we pull out for the islands."

The men made sure the boys were securely bound, then disappeared. Frank and Joe struggled furiously at their bonds, but the wires would not budge. They only cut more deeply into their flesh. To keep their minds off the fate awaiting them, the brothers discussed the case with Jezro.

"What about the pigeons in the woods?" Frank asked. "Why was one shot, Jezro?"

"It wasn't supposed to be. I did that. I didn't know it was one of our birds. But I guess my shootin' days are over. We're goners now," he added despondently.

As night descended, the man's terror grew almost to hysteria. He moaned and babbled as though losing his reason. The Hardys called back and forth, to keep up their hopes, though their spirits had never been lower. Any minute now the wolves might be released.

Suddenly a distant sound pierced the stillness. The wailing siren! The helicopter was coming! Were the gang making their getaway from their North Woods hideout?

The siren was answered by the loud blast of the one located at the gang's cabin. A few minutes later the beams of a searchlight were lighting the sky above the trees.

The boys could hear Krack and his gang coming on the run to roll up the canvas camouflage on the landing field. Presently through the trees the boys could see the lights around the rim of the clearing.

They strained to look upward as the craft hovered overhead, and watched as it gently touched the ground. As its door swung open, the smugglers rushed to meet the pilot.

To the boys' joy and amazement, they saw Fenton Hardy and several state troopers alighting from the chopper.

"Don't move, any of you!" came an order from Mr. Hardy which rang through the silent woods.

Trippek and Krack stood staring, unbelieving. Then Renaldo sprang toward the lights. If he could plunge the place into darkness, he and his friends might escape.

An officer's gun clipped a bit of foliage just above the man's head, and the leader of the gang suddenly seemed to change his mind.

Then they heard their father demanding angrily what they had done with his sons. A moment later the detective was snipping the wires that bound Joe and Frank. Then, though their arms and legs were cramped, the boys had the supreme pleasure of helping the troopers manacle the criminals and march them to the helicopter. Joe and Frank, with their father and two of the police officers, stayed behind to round up Jezro and the remaining lesser members of the gang, and to tie up the wolves. A police helicopter would return to pick them up later.

"Gosh, Dad, you came just in time!" Joe cried gleefully, when the boys had a chance to speak to him alone.

"How did you get loose?" Frank asked him.

"I was never caught."

"What?"

"I got Saber before he got me. Then I made my way to Krack's cabin and overheard him talking to Haxon on short wave. He mentioned that the helicopter was hidden at the Beekman farm. Then I got a message through to Sam Radley, who was secretly tailing us all the time to take over if I needed him. I told him to let himself be captured by the gang, while I went to notify the troopers. I even gave him the gas gun to make Krack and his crew think it was I they had nabbed."

"So Sam fooled them!"

"Right. Fortunately for me, Krack and Jezro didn't know what I looked like. I hurried to get help from the state troopers to raid the old barn and capture the helicopter and the pilot."

"What about Haxon?" Frank asked.

"I notified the Coast Guard. They seized the yacht and have Haxon in the brig. Which, by the way, solves my mystery of the stolen currency and the smuggled munitions. A list of the thieves and gunrunners was found in Haxon's cabin."

"And our mystery is solved, too," Frank said, telling what Jezro had revealed.

The Hardys picked their way through the woods to Krack's cabin, where they found and released Sam Radley.

What the gangsters had not already told was learned from records found in a desk. Two airplane motors and other stolen equipment were found and brought out of the woods the next day.

Solved, also, was one of the questions that had puzzled Frank and Joe ever since the day they had seen the airplane motor in the shack. The engines were taken apart and brought piecemeal from the house where Frank had been imprisoned. A crack mechanic, one of the gang, had reassembled the engines in the forest shack.

Bayport buzzed with the news of the Hardys' latest exploit. Many people prophesied that another mystery would soon come their way. It did and was titled *The Secret of Wildcat Swamp*.

The following night Mrs. Hardy invited her sons' special friends to a party at their home to celebrate the successful wind-up of the case.

Soon the living room was filled with music and chatter. Even Aunt Gertrude, who was serving sandwiches, was feeling mellow.

"Thank goodness those cutthroats were caught," she said, proud of her nephews and their father. "Did you get your—our—money back, Chester?"

Chet's mouth was filled with a ham sandwich, so he could only nod the good news. Then he swallowed and said, "And my uncle's rifles, too."

Mr. Hardy came in to report more good news. The men in the speedboat and the launch had been arrested.

"And our pilot friend Jack Wayne was found in Haxon's Caribbean headquarters," he said. "He and some other pilots had been kidnapped with their planes by stowaways and were being held to train pilots for the subversive armies. Wayne's on his way back to Bayport right now."

The boys sent up a cheer. When it subsided, the detective went on, "Frank and Joe have been given a reward for their part in the capture of Red Mike, Renaldo, Krack, and Trippek."

Again the guests cheered.

"What are you going to do with your reward?" Chet asked the Hardys.

The brothers grinned. "We'll use some of it to help pay for all of that camping equipment you charged," Joe said.

Order Form
New revised editions of
THE BOBBSEY TWINS®

In *hardcover* at your local bookseller OR
simply mail in this handy order coupon and start your collection today!

Please send me the following Bobbsey Twins titles I've checked below.

AVOID DELAYS   Please Print Order Form Clearly

❏	1	Of Lakeport	($5.99)	448-09071-6
❏	2	Adventure in the Country	($5.95)	448-09072-4
❏	6	On a Houseboat	($4.95)	448-09099-6
❏	7	Mystery at Meadowbrook	($4.50)	448-09100-3
❏	8	Big Adventure at Home	($4.50)	448-09134-8

Own the original exciting
BOBBSEY TWINS® ADVENTURE STORIES
still available:

❏13   Visit to the Great West   ($4.50)   448-08013-3

**VISIT PUTNAM BERKLEY ONLINE
ON THE INTERNET: http://www.putnam.com/berkley**

Payable in U.S. funds. No cash accepted. Postage & handling: $3.50 for one book. $1.00 for each additional. Maximum postage $8.50. Prices, postage and handling charges may change without notice. Visa, Amex, MasterCard call 1-800-788-6262, ext. 1, or fax 1-201-933-2316.

Or, check above books
and send this order form to:

**The Putnam Publishing Group
P.O. Box 12289, Dept. B
Newark, NJ 07101-5289**

Please allow 4-6 weeks for delivery.
Foreign and Canadian delivery 8-12 weeks

Book Total	$ _____
Applicable Sales Tax (CA, NJ, NY, GST Can.)	$ _____
Postage & Handling	$ _____
Total Amount Due	$ _____

The Bobbsey Twins® Series is a trademark
of Simon & Schuster, Inc. and is registered
in the United States Patent and Trademark Office.

Bill my: ❏ Visa ❏ MasterCard ❏ Amex _____(expires)

Card#_____
                                                    ($10 minimum)

Daytime Phone # _____

Signature_____

Or enclosed is my: ❏ check ❏ money order
SHIP TO:
Name _____
Address _____
City _____ State _____Zip _____
BILL TO:
Name _____
Address _____
City _____ State _____Zip _____